Lucia lifted her chin. "Where's the bedroom?"

Surprise flared silver in his eyes and his mouth quirked in a small smile. "You are constantly amazing me."

She ignored the warmth that flared through her at his praise. "Don't patronize me, Angelo."

"Trust me, I am not. Perhaps tragedy has made you stronger, Lucia, for you have far more spirit now than I ever gave you credit for when we were children."

"Yes, I do." Tragedy *had* made her stronger. She was glad he saw it. "The bedroom," she prompted, and he smiled faintly even as he watched her, still wary.

"Are you sure about this?"

"Why shouldn't I be?"

"A decision like this should not be made in the heat of the moment—"

"And it's not the heat of the moment right now," she answered. Still he stared at her, his eyes dark and considering.

"I don't," he finally said in a low voice, "want to hurt you."

"You won't," she said. This time she wouldn't let him. She knew what she wanted, what to expect. This time she would be the one to walk away."

Dear Reader,

We have exciting news! As I'm sure you've noticed, the Harlequin Presents books you know and love have a brand-new look, starting this month. They look *sensational!* Don't you agree?

But don't worry—nothing else about the Presents books has changed. You'll still find eight unforgettable love stories every month, with alpha heroes, empowered heroines and stunning international destinations all topped with passion and a sensual attraction that burns as brightly as ever.

Don't miss any of this month's exciting reads:

I hope you're as pleased with our new look as we are. Drop by www.Harlequin.com to let us know what you think.

Joanne Grant
Senior Editor
Harlequin Presents

Kate Hewitt

AN INHERITANCE OF SHAME

SICILY'S
CORRETTI
DYNASTY

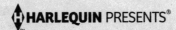

HARLEQUIN PRESENTS®

Recycling programs for this product may not exist in your area.

ISBN-13: 978-0-373-13168-6

AN INHERITANCE OF SHAME

Copyright © 2013 by Harlequin Books S.A.

Special thanks and acknowledgment are given to Kate Hewitt for her contribution to Sicily's Corretti Dynasty series

Printed in U.S.A.

The more powerful the family…the darker the secrets!

Introducing the Correttis—Sicily's most scandalous family!
Behind the closed doors of their opulent palazzo, ruthless desire and the
lethal Coretti charm are alive and well.
Harlequin Presents invites you to step over the threshold and enter the
Correttis' dark and dazzling world….

The Empire

Young, rich and notoriously handsome, the Correttis' legendary exploits
regularly feature in Sicily's tabloid pages!

The Scandal

But how long can their reputations withstand the glaring heat of the
spotlight before their family's secrets are exposed?

The Legacy

Once nearly destroyed by the secrets cloaking their thirst for power, the
new generation of Correttis are riding high again—and no disgrace or
scandal will stand in their way….

Sicily's Corretti Dynasty

8 volumes to collect—you won't want to miss out!

Other titles by Kate Hewitt available in ebook:

To Gabri—thanks for all your help with Italian phrases. I don't know what I'd do without you! Love, K.

CHAPTER ONE

IT WAS HIS. All his. *Almost* his, for tomorrow he had an appointment to sign the papers transferring the ownership of the Corretti Hotel Palermo from Corretti Enterprises to Corretti International. Angelo Corretti's mouth twisted at the irony. From one Corretti to another. Or not.

Slowly he strolled through the hotel lobby, watching the bellhops catch sight of him, their eyes widening before they straightened to attention. A middle-aged woman at the concierge desk eyed him apprehensively, clearly waiting to spring into action if summoned. He hadn't been formally introduced to any of the hotel staff, but he had no doubt they knew who he was. He'd been in and out of the Corretti offices for nearly a week, arranging meetings with the major shareholders who had no choice but to hand over the reins of the flagship hotel in view of their CEO's absence and Angelo's controlling shares.

It had, in the end, all been so gloriously simple. Leave the Correttis alone for a little while and they'd tear themselves apart. They just couldn't help it.

'Sir? Signor…Corretti?' The concierge finally approached him, her heels clicking across the marble floor of the soaring foyer. Angelo heard how she stumbled over his name, because of course everyone knew the

Correttis here, and in all of Sicily. They were the most powerful and scandalous family in southern Italy. And he wasn't one of them.

Except he was.

He felt his mouth twist downwards as that all too familiar and futile rage coursed through him. He was one of them, but he had never—and never would be— acknowledged as one, even if everyone knew the truth of his birth. Even if everyone in the village he'd grown up in, from the time he was a little boy and barely un- derstood it himself, had known he was Carlo Corretti's bastard and made his life hell because of it.

He turned to the concierge, forcing his mouth upwards into a smile. 'Yes?'

'Is there anything I can do for you?' she asked, and he saw the uncertainty in her eyes, the fear that he'd come in here and sweep it all clean. And part of him was tempted to do just that. Every single person who worked here had been loyal to the family he despised and was determined to ruin. Why shouldn't he fire them all, bring in his own people?

'No, thank you, Natalia.' He'd glanced at her discreet, silver-plated name tag before meeting her worried gaze with a faint smile. 'I'll just go to my room.' He'd booked the penthouse suite for tonight, intending to savour stay- ing in the best room of his enemy's best hotel. The room he knew for a fact was reserved almost exclusively for Matteo Corretti's use, except since the debacle of the called-off Corretti/Battaglia wedding, Matteo was no- where to be seen. He wouldn't be using the suite even if he could, which from tomorrow he couldn't.

No Corretti, save for himself, would ever stay in this hotel again.

'Certainly, Signor Corretti.' She spoke his name more

surely now, but it felt like a hollow victory. He'd always been a Corretti, had claimed the name for his own even though the man who had fathered him had never admitted to it or him. Even though using that name had earned him more black eyes and bloody noses than he cared to remember. It was his, damn it, and he'd earned it.

He'd earned all of this.

With one last cool smile for the concierge, he turned towards the bank of gleaming lifts and pressed the button for the penthouse. It was nearly midnight, and the foyer was deserted except for a skeleton staff. The streets outside one of Palermo's busiest squares had emptied out, and Angelo hadn't seen anyone on his walk here from his temporary offices a few blocks away.

Yet as he soared upwards towards the hotel's top floor and its glittering, panoramic view of the city and harbour, Angelo knew he was too wired and restless to sleep. Sleep, at the best times, had always been difficult; he often only caught two or three hours in a night, and that not always consecutively. The rest of the time he worked or exercised, anything to keep his body and brain moving, doing.

The doors opened directly into the suite that covered the entire top floor. Angelo stepped inside, his narrowed gaze taking in all the luxurious details: the marble floor, the crystal chandelier, the expensive antiques and art. The lights had been turned down and he glimpsed a wide king-size bed in the suite's master bedroom, the navy silk duvet turned down to reveal the six hundred thread count sheets underneath.

He dropped his key card onto a side table and loosened his tie, shed his jacket. He felt the beginnings of a headache, the throbbing at his temples telling him he'd be facing a migraine in a couple of hours. Migraines and insomnia were just two of the prices he'd had to pay for how hard he'd worked, how much he'd achieved, and he paid them willingly. He'd pay just about anything to be where he was, who he was. Successful, powerful, with the ability to pull the sumptuous rug out from under the Correttis' feet.

He strolled through the suite, the lights of the city visible and glittering from the floor-to-ceiling windows. The living area was elegant if a bit too stuffy for his taste, with some fussy little chairs and tables, a few ridiculous-looking urns. He'd have a refit of the whole hotel first thing, he decided as he plucked a grape from the bowl of fresh fruit on the coffee table, another fussy piece of furniture, with fluted, gold-leaf edges. He'd bring this place up to date, modern and cutting edge. It had been relying on the distinctly tattered Corretti name and a faded elegance for far too long.

Restless, his head starting to really pound, he continued to prowl through the suite, knowing he wouldn't be able to sleep yet unwilling to sit down and work. This was the eve of his victory after all. He should be celebrating.

Unfortunately he had no one to celebrate with in this town. He hadn't made any friends here in the eighteen years he'd called Sicily home, only enemies.

You made one friend.

The thought slid into his mind, surprising and sweet, and he stilled his restless pacing of the suite's living area.

Lucia. He tried not to think of her, because thinking of her was remembering and remembering made him wonder. Wish. *Regret.*

And he never regretted anything. He wouldn't regret the one night he'd spent in her arms, burying himself so deep inside her he'd almost forgotten who he was—and who he wasn't.

For a few blissful hours Lucia Anturri, the neighbour's daughter he'd ignored and appreciated in turns, with the startling blue eyes that mirrored her heart, had made him forget all the anger and pain and emptiness he'd ever felt.

And then he'd slipped away from her while she was sleeping and gone back to his life in New York, to the man of purpose and determination and anger that he'd always be, because damn it, he didn't *want* to forget.

Not even for one night.

Even more restless now, that old anger surging through him, Angelo jerked open the buttons of his shirt. He'd take a long, hot shower. Sometimes that helped with the headaches, and at least it was something to do.

He was in the process of shedding his shirt as he came into the bedroom and to an abrupt halt. A bucket of ice with a bottle of champagne chilling inside was by the bed—and so was a woman.

Lucia froze at the sight of the half-dressed man in front of her, three freshly laundered towels pressed to her hard-beating heart.

Angelo.

She knew, had always known, that she would see him again, and occasionally she'd embroidered ridiculous, romantic fantasies about how it would happen. Stupid, schoolgirl dreams. She hadn't done that for years though, and she'd never imagined this.

Running into him without a second's notice, totally unprepared—

She'd heard whispers that he was back in Sicily but

she had assumed they were, as they'd always been, mere rumours, and she'd never expected to see him here.

From just one shocked glimpse of him standing there, his hair rumpled and his shirt half undone, she knew he didn't recognise her. Meanwhile in the space of a few seconds she was reliving every glorious and agonising moment she'd spent with him that one night seven years ago, the feel of his satiny skin, the desperate press of his lips against hers.

Such thoughts were clearly the furthest from his mind. His eyes had narrowed, his lips thinned, and he looked angry. She recognised that look, for God knew she'd seen it enough over the fraught years of their childhood. Yet even angry he was beautiful, the most beautiful man she'd ever known.

Known and loved.

Swallowing, she pushed that most unhelpful thought away. She hadn't seen Angelo in seven years. She didn't love him any more, and she absolutely knew he'd never loved her.

Which, of course, shouldn't hurt all this time later, yet in that unguarded moment as she stared at him, his shirt hanging open to reveal the taut, golden expanse of his chest, she knew it did.

Angelo arched an eyebrow, obviously annoyed, clearly waiting. For what? An apology? Did he expect her to do the little chambermaid stammering act and scurry away?

Two desires, both deep-seated, warred within her. On one hand she felt like telling Angelo Corretti exactly what she thought of him for sneaking out of her bed seven years ago. Except she didn't even know what that was, because she thought of Angelo in so many ways. Desire and despair. Hope and hatred. Love and loss.

In any case, the far more sensible impulse she had was

to leave this room before he recognised her, before any awful, awkward reunion scenarios could play out. They may have been childhood friends, he may have been her first and only lover, but she was next to nothing to him, and always had been—a shaming fact she did not need reminding of tonight.

'I'm sorry,' she said, lowering her head just a little so her hair fell in front of her face. 'I was just getting your room ready for the night. I'll be out of your way.'

She started to move past him, her head still lowered, hating the ache this simple, terrible exchange opened up inside her. It was an ache she'd had for so long that she'd become numb to it, learned to live with it the way you might a missing limb or a permanent scar. Yet now, in Angelo's uncaring presence, she felt it throb painfully to life and for a second, furious with herself, she had to blink back tears.

She was just about to slip past him when his hand curled around her arm, jolting her so hard and deep she almost stumbled.

'Wait.'

She stilled, her heart hammering, her breath caught in her chest. Angelo let go of her arm and walked towards the bed.

'I'm celebrating, you know,' he said, but he didn't sound like he was. He sounded as sardonic and cynical as he'd ever been. Lucia tensed, her back to him, her face angled away. He still didn't recognise her, and that realisation gave her equal parts relief and deep disappointment.

'Why don't you celebrate with me,' he continued, clearly a command, and she stiffened. Was this what he'd become? The kind of man who solicited the housekeeping? 'Just a drink,' he clarified, and now he sounded coolly amused as he popped the cork on the complimentary bottle of champagne that always came with the penthouse suite. 'Since nobody else is here.'

Lucia turned around slowly, her whole body rigid. She had no idea how to act. What to say. This had gone on way too long for her to keep pretending she was a stranger, and yet—

Maybe that's what she was to him now. A stranger.

He was pouring the champagne into two crystal flutes, his mouth twisted downwards, and something in the shuttered bleakness of his expression called to that ache deep inside her, the ache she'd been trying so hard and for so long to ignore. When he looked like that it reminded her of when he'd shown up on her doorstep seven years ago, when he'd stared at her so bleakly, so blankly, and his voice had broken as he'd confessed, *'He's dead, Lucia. And I don't feel anything.'*

She hadn't thought then; she'd just drawn him inside by the hand, led him to the shabby little living room of the house she'd grown up in and where she then lived alone.

And started something—a single night—that had changed her life for ever.

She swallowed now, forced herself to lift her chin and look him in the eye. She saw him tense, *felt* it, one hand still outstretched, a flute of fizzing champagne clasped between his long, lean fingers.

'All right, Angelo,' she said, and thankfully her voice remained steady. 'I'll have a drink with you.'

Angelo stood completely motionless, his hand still outstretched. The only sound in the room was the gentle fizz of the champagne's bubbles popping against the sides of the crystal flute and his own suddenly ragged breathing.

Lucia.

How could he not have recognised her? How could he have not known her from the moment he'd seen her in his suite? The first thought that seared his brain now was the completely irrelevant realisation of how *blue* her eyes were, so startling against her dark hair and olive skin. How wide and clear and open they'd always been, open to him.

Then chasing the heels of that poignant memory was a far more bitter realisation—and with it a dawning fury.

'You work for them? Those *sciacalli*?'

Her chin tilted up a notch and those blue, blue eyes flashed even bluer. 'If you mean am I employed at this hotel, then the answer is yes.'

Another thing he'd forgotten: the low, husky timbre of her voice, sounding sensual and smoky and still so tender and sweet. He had a sudden, painfully clear recollection of her asking him in that same low voice what he'd expected to feel that night, the night of his father's funeral, what he'd wanted to feel. He'd answered in a ragged gulp that just stopped short of a sob, *'Satisfaction. Happiness. Something. I just feel empty.'*

She hadn't replied, just put her arms around him, and he'd turned into her embrace, burying his head in the sweet curve of her neck before his lips had found hers, seeking and needing the total acceptance and understanding she'd always so freely given.

And now she worked for the Correttis? The family who had made his childhood a living hell? He shook his head slowly, his head throbbing so hard his vision blurred. 'So what, you're on your knees for them? Scrubbing their filth, bobbing a curtsey when they come by? What happened to your promise, Lucia?'

'My promise,' she repeated, her voice completely expressionless.

He pressed one fist against his temple, closed his eyes briefly against the pain that thundered in his head—and in his heart. 'Do you not even remember? You promised me you'd never even talk to them—'

'As a matter of fact, Angelo, I don't talk to them. I'm a chambermaid, one of dozens. They don't even know my name.'

'So that excuses—'

'Do you really want to talk about excuses?' she asked levelly, and he opened his eyes, pressed his fist harder against his temple. Damn it, his head hurt. And even in the midst of his shock and pain he recognised how ridiculous he was being. She'd made those silly promises when she was a child, a girl of no more than eleven or twelve. He remembered the moment, stupidly. He'd been jumped on his way back to school, beaten bloody but he'd come up swinging as always. She'd been waiting on her doorstep, her heart in her eyes. She'd tried to comfort him, and in his hurt pride and anger he'd shrugged her off.

But she kept trying—she'd always kept *trying*—and he'd let her press an ice pack to his eye and wipe the blood away. He'd caught her looking at him, her eyes so wide and serious, and he'd grabbed her wrist and demanded roughly, *'Promise. Promise you'll never speak to them, or like them, or even work for them—'*

She'd blinked once, twice, and then answered in a voice that was low and husky even then. *'I promise.'*

No, he didn't want to talk about excuses now. He knew he didn't have any. Seven years since he'd left her in bed and he still felt that needling pinprick of guilt when he allowed himself to feel it—or anything.

Not that he'd allowed himself to think of her often.

By eight o'clock the morning after they'd slept together he'd already been on a plane back to New York, having resolutely shoved her out of his mind.

And now she was back, and the memories cascaded over him, a tidal wave of unexpected emotion he had no desire to feel.

He shut his eyes again, his fist still pressed to his temple.

'You're getting a migraine, aren't you,' she said quietly, and he opened his eyes, dropped his hand. He'd used to get headaches even as a child, and she'd given him aspirin, rubbed his temples when he'd let her.

'It doesn't matter.'

'What doesn't matter? That you have a headache, or that I work for the Correttis?'

'You don't work for them any more.'

Her eyes widened for one fraught second and he knew she thought he was firing her. 'I own the hotel now,' he explained flatly, and he heard her slight indrawn breath.

'Congratulations,' she said after a tiny pause, and he couldn't tell a thing from her tone. She seemed so different now, so calm and controlled, so *cold*. So unlike the warm, generous person she'd been, giving him her body and maybe even her heart in the course of a single night—

No, not her heart. Long ago he'd wondered briefly if she had romanticised their one encounter, thought she might have because of their shared history. He'd worried that she might have expected more from him, things he knew he wasn't capable of, couldn't give.

Looking at her impassive face now he knew any uneasy concerns he had once had were completely unfounded, and he wasn't even surprised. Of course Lucia had moved on.

'Do you have any tablets?' she asked calmly, and the pain was bad enough that he answered her.

'In my wash kit, in my bag.'

She slipped past him, and he inhaled her scent as she went by. He sank onto the edge of the bed, the flute of champagne still dangling from his fingers. Distantly over the pounding in his brain he heard her moving about, unzipping his suitcase.

A few minutes later she came back in and knelt by his side. 'Let me take this,' she said, and plucked the champagne from his fingers. 'And give you this.' She handed him a glass of water and two tablets. 'I checked the dosage. It said two?'

He nodded, and he felt her hand wrap around his as she guided the glass to his lips. Even through the pain pounding in his head he felt a spark of awareness blaze from his fingers all the way to his groin. He remembered how sweet and yielding she'd been in his arms, without even so much as a word spoken between them. But then Lucia had always been sweet and yielding, always been willing to take care of him, even when he'd pushed her away again and again.

Clearly she'd changed, for she pulled her hand away from his, and he stamped down on that spark.

'Thank you,' he said gruffly. They may have shared one desperate, passionate night, but he knew there was nothing between them now. There couldn't be.

Lucia sat back on her heels and watched Angelo struggle with himself, as he so often did. Feeling weak and hating to show it. And her, wanting to help him and hating how he always pushed her away. The story of both of their lives.

A story she was done with, she told herself now. Seeing Angelo again might have opened up that ache inside her, but she wasn't going to do anything about it. She wasn't going to be stupid about it, even though part of her, just as before, as always, yearned towards him and whatever little he could give.

No. He'd wrecked her before, and broken not just her heart but her whole self. Shattered her into pieces, and she wouldn't allow even a hairline crack to appear now. It had taken years to put herself together again, to feel strong if not actually ever complete.

She rose, picking up the towels she'd dropped when she'd gone for his pills. 'Will you be all right?' she said, making it not so much a question as a statement.

'I'm fine,' he said, the words a growl, and she knew he was already regretting that little display of vulnerability.

'Then I'll leave you to it,' she said, and Angelo didn't answer. She took a few steps and then stopped, her back to him, one hand on the doorframe, suddenly unwilling to go so simply. So easily. Words bubbled up, bottled in her throat. Words that threatened to spill out of the hurt and pain she felt even now, so many years later. The pain and hurt she didn't want him to see, because if he saw it he'd know how much she'd cared. How weak she'd been—and still was.

She swallowed it all down, those words and worse ones, broken, wounded words about a grief so very deep and raw that he knew nothing about. She couldn't tell him tonight.

Maybe she wouldn't ever tell him. Did he really need to know? Wouldn't it be better to simply move on, or at least to let him think she had moved on?

'Lucia?' Angelo said, and it was a question although

what he was asking she didn't know. *What do you want? Why are you still here?*

'I'm going,' she said, and then she forced herself to walk out of the suite without looking back.

CHAPTER TWO

ANGELO FINGERED THE typewritten list of the hotel's employees that lay on his desk. Matteo's desk, because there had been no time to change anything since signing the papers on the hotel this morning. He'd gone directly from the meeting of unhappy shareholders to here, sweeping into his rival's office and claiming it as his own.

His mouth twisted as he glanced at the tabloid headline he'd left up on his laptop. Not that he actually read those rags, but this one blazed bad news about the Correttis. Alessandro Corretti was meant to have wed Alessia Battaglia, but she'd run off with his cousin Matteo at the very last second. Angelo smiled grimly. The chaos that had ensued was devastating for his half-brothers and cousins, but good news for him.

With Matteo out of the way and the other Correttis scrambling to make sense of the chaos, he could saunter in and take another slice of the Corretti pie, starting with the docklands regeneration. Antonio Battaglia, the Minister of Trade and Housing as well as Alessia's father, would be all too willing to consider his bid, since he was already funding a housing project in the area. Angelo had made initial overtures, and planned to cement the deal this week.

He glanced back at the list of employees. *Anturri,*

Lucia was the first name under the housekeeping section. As soon as he'd arrived back at the hotel he'd pulled up the employee files and seen that Lucia had been working here for seven years, the entire length of time since he'd last seen her.

Why did that hurt?

No, it didn't hurt. Annoyed him, perhaps. From his bed to making the Correttis'. Had she had a moment's pause, a second's worth of regret, before she took a job working for the family he hated, the family who had rejected him even as his association with them had defined and nearly destroyed his life?

Or had she just not cared?

Yet Lucia had *always* cared. She'd always been there when they were children, waiting for him to come home, ready to bathe his cuts or just make him smile with a stupid story or joke. More often than not he'd pushed her away, too angry to accept her offers of friendship. *Mi cucciola*, he'd called her. My puppy. An endearment but also a barb because she *had* been like a puppy, dogging his heels, pleading for a pat on the head. Sometimes he'd given it, sometimes he'd ignored her and sometimes he'd sent her away.

Yet still she'd come back, her heart in her eyes just like it had been the night he'd shown up at her door, too numb to feel anything except the sudden, desperate passion she'd awoken in him when she'd taken him in her arms.

Guilt needled him again as he thought of that night, how he'd slipped from her bed before dawn without a single word of farewell. He should have said goodbye, at least. Considering their history, their shared childhood, she'd deserved that much. Even if it didn't seem like it mattered to her any more. It mattered, annoyingly, to him.

He stood up, pacing the spacious confines of the office with his usual restlessness. He should be feeling victorious now, savagely satisfied, but he only felt uneasy, restless, the remnants of his migraine mocking him.

He'd spent another sleepless night battling memories as well as his migraine. For seven years he'd schooled himself not to think of that night, to act as if it hadn't happened. Yet last night in the throes of pain he'd been weak, and he'd remembered.

Remembered the sweet slide of her lips against his, the way she'd drawn him to herself, curling around him, *accepting* him in a way he'd never been before or since. How he'd felt tears spring to his eyes when he'd joined his body with hers, how absolutely right and whole that moment had felt.

Idiotic. He was *not* a romantic, and a single encounter—poignant as it may have been—didn't mean anything. It obviously hadn't meant anything to Lucia, who had seemed completely unmoved by his appearance last night. And if *Lucia*, who had hero-worshipped him as a child, could be indifferent and even cold towards him now, than surely he could act the same. Feel the same.

In any case he had too many other things to accomplish to waste even a second on Lucia Anturri or what had happened between them. Nothing would happen between them now. He'd come back to Sicily for one purpose only: to ruin the Correttis. To finally have his revenge.

Determinedly Angelo pulled the phone towards him. It was time to call Antonio Battaglia, and start carving up that Corretti pie.

* * *

Lucia felt the throb in her temples and wondered if head-aches could be contagious. She'd had one since she'd left Angelo in the penthouse suite last night, and spent a sleepless night trying *not* to remember their one night together.

Yet far worse than the pain in her head was the ache seeing Angelo had opened up in her heart. No tablet or pill would help that. Swallowing hard, she pushed the trolley of fresh linens and cleaning supplies down the corridor. She had to finish all the third-floor rooms by lunchtime. She had to forget about Angelo.

How can you forget him when you haven't told him?

Last night, she knew, hadn't been the right time. She'd even half convinced herself that he need never know the consequence of their one night together. What point was there, really, in raking up the past? It wouldn't change things. It wouldn't change him.

And yet Lucia knew if the positions had been some-how reversed she would want to know. Yet could she really assume that Angelo would feel the same? And if she did tell him, and he shrugged it off as irrelevant, wouldn't that break her heart all over again? Just one brief conversation with him last night and already she felt it starting to splinter.

She was almost finished the third floor, her head and heart both aching, when she heard the muffled sobs com-ing from the supply room at the end of the hall. Frown-ing, Lucia pushed open the door and her heart twisted at the sight inside the little room stacked with towels and industrial-size bottles of cleaner.

'Maria.'

Maria Dibona, another chambermaid, looked up at her with tear-streaked eyes. *'Scusi, scusi,'* she said, wiping at her eyes. Lucia reached for a box of tissues used to supply the hotel bathrooms and handed her one. 'Is it Stefano?'

Maria nodded. Lucia knew her son had left Sicily for a life in Naples, and his sudden defection had broken his mother's heart.

'I'm sorry, Maria.' She put her arm around the older woman. 'Have you been in touch?'

'He hasn't even called.' Maria pressed the tissue to her eyes. 'How is a mother to live, not knowing if her son is healthy or not? Alive or not?'

'He will call,' Lucia murmured. 'He loves you, you know. Even if he doesn't always show it.' She meant the words for Maria, yet she felt their mocking echo in herself. Hadn't she told herself the same thing after Angelo had left? Hadn't she tried to convince herself that he would call or write, *reach* her, even as the heaviness in her heart told her otherwise?

When she'd rolled over and seen the smooth expanse of empty sheet next to her she'd known Angelo wasn't coming back. Wasn't writing, calling or keeping in touch in any way…no matter how desperately she tried to believe otherwise.

Maria blew her nose. 'He was such a good boy. Why did he have to leave?'

Lucia just shook her head and squeezed the woman's shoulders. She had no answers, no real comfort to give besides her own understanding and sympathy. She'd lived too long and experienced too much heartache to offer anyone pat answers. There were none.

She heard the sound of someone striding down the hall, someone walking with purpose and determination. Instinctively she stiffened, and then shock iced through as an all too familiar face appeared around the door of the little supply cupboard.

'Lucia.'

She straightened and Maria lurched upright, dabbing her face frantically. '*Scusi, scusi*, Signor Corretti…'

Angelo waved a hand in quick dismissal of the other woman. His grey-green eyes blazed into Lucia's. 'I need to speak with you.'

'Very well.' Lucia hid her trembling hands in her apron. She hadn't expected to see him again so soon, or even at all. She had no idea what he intended to say, but she knew she wasn't ready for the conversation.

'In my office.' Angelo turned away, and Lucia glanced back at Maria, whose eyes had rounded in surprise. Maria was no gossip, but Lucia knew the news would still spread. Angelo Corretti had summoned her to his office for a private conversation. All the old memories and rumours would be raked up.

Closing her eyes briefly, she followed Angelo out into the corridor. They didn't speak as they stepped into a lift that took them to the second-to-top floor that housed the hotel's corporate offices, yet Lucia was all too achingly aware of the man next to her, the suppressed tension in every taut line of his lean body, the anger apparent in the tightness of his square jaw. She tried not to look at him, because if she looked at him she'd drink him in and she knew her need and want would be visible in her eyes, all too obvious to him.

Still. Still she felt that welling up of longing for him, a hopeless yearning that had her almost swaying towards him. It infuriated her, that her body and even her heart could want a man who had so little regard for her. At least her mind was strong. She straightened, lifted her chin. Angelo would never know how much he'd hurt her.

The lift doors pinged open and Lucia felt her cheeks warm as Angelo strode past a receptionist whose jaw dropped when she saw Lucia in her standard grey maid's uniform, complete with frilly apron and ridiculous cap, follow him into his office like a scolded schoolgirl…or a summoned mistress.

No, she wouldn't think like that. Couldn't, even if everyone else would. Again.

Angelo strode towards the floor-to-ceiling windows with a view of Palermo's harbour, one hand braced against the glass, his back to her. Lucia waited, her heart pounding even as her hungry gaze swept over him, the long, muscular stretch of back, the narrow hips, the powerful legs. The elegant, expensive suit that reminded her just how out of her league he was now.

Angelo swung around suddenly to face her, his eyes narrowed. 'Why did you start working at this hotel?'

Lucia blinked. 'Because I needed a job.'

'Surely you could have found a suitable position somewhere else.'

She drew herself up even though she felt like curling into a protective ball, hiding her hurts. How could he be angry about her *job*? 'Are you still angry that I broke my promise, Angelo?' she asked, an edge to her voice. 'That seems rather hypocritical.'

'I didn't make any promises,' he said flatly, and she drew in one short, sharp breath. Felt the truth of his words cut her as if he were wielding a sword.

'I know that.'

'So why did you?'

She gritted her teeth, forced herself to sound calm. Strong. 'I told you, I needed a job. Did you really call me up here to ask me that—'

'Did you even think of that promise you made, Lucia?'

he cut her off harshly. His hands clenched into fists at his sides. 'Did you think of me?'

Every day. She drew a painful breath into her lungs. 'Did you think of me, Angelo?' she asked quietly, knowingly, and he swung away again, his silence answer enough.

Lucia waited, her hands clenched in the folds of her apron. A minute ticked by in taut silence, and then another, and Angelo still didn't speak.

'Who was that woman you were with?' he asked suddenly, and she blinked in surprise.

'Her name is Maria Dibona. She works here, with me.'

'I gathered that.' Angelo turned towards her, but she couldn't tell anything from his face besides the fact that he still seemed angry. But then Angelo had always seemed angry, except perhaps for when he'd been sad. And the few times he'd made her laugh, when they were children…precious memories she kept locked away, deep inside. Memories she couldn't let herself think about now. 'Why was she crying?' he asked, and she shrugged.

'Her son has left suddenly for Naples. She misses him.'

Angelo said nothing for a moment, but his eyes blazed into hers and his mouth twisted downwards. 'And you were comforting her?'

Where was this going? 'Trying to. Sometimes there's very little comfort to be had.'

He didn't answer, but she saw a flash of recognition in his eyes and she knew he thought she'd been talking about them. What little *them* there was. And had she? Perhaps. Perhaps she wasn't above such a sly implication.

'You still live in Caltarione,' he said suddenly, a statement, and she raised her eyebrows.

'Obviously you must know that, since you've looked

at my employee file. What is this about, Angelo? Why have you brought me up here?'

She saw, to her surprise, a faint flush touch his cheekbones. He glanced down at some papers on his desk. 'We were friends once, weren't we?'

Once, not now. His meaning was clear. 'As children, yes,' she said flatly.

'I want to know what has happened to you in these past years.'

'Oh, really? Funny, then, that you never called or wrote. Not a postcard or email or anything. If you wanted to catch up on old times, Angelo, I'm sure you could have found a way other than summoning me to your office like some scolded schoolgirl.'

His blush deepened, and his eyes glittered. 'I didn't—'

'Didn't think of me once in the past seven years while you were away becoming a billionaire? How surprising. And yet you're angry because I took a job working for the Correttis.' She shook her head. 'You may not have made any promises, but you're still a hypocrite.'

'You're angry with me,' he said, and she forced herself to laugh, the sound hard and humourless.

'Angry? That takes too much effort. I *was* angry, yes, and I'm annoyed you think you can order me around now. But if you think I'm hurt because you stole from my bed—' She stopped suddenly, her breath catching in her chest, and swallowed hard. She knew she couldn't continue, couldn't maintain the charade that what had happened seven years ago hadn't utterly broken her.

So she simply stared, her chin tilted at a determinedly haughty angle, everything in her willing Angelo to believe that she didn't care about him. That he hadn't hurt her. Let him believe she was only angry; at least it hid the agony of grief she couldn't bear to have exposed.

'I'm sorry, Lucia,' Angelo said abruptly, and Lucia could only stare. He didn't *sound* sorry.

'For what?' she asked after a taut moment when neither of them spoke.

'For...' He paused, a muscle flickering in his jaw, his eyes shadowed with some dark emotion. 'For leaving you like that.' Lucia let out a shuddering breath. She'd never expected an apology, even one so grudgingly given. She didn't speak. Angelo stared.

'Aren't you going to say anything?' he finally demanded.

'What do you want me to say?'

'You could accept my apology, to start.'

'Why should I?'

Angelo's jaw dropped, which would have made her laugh save for the leaden weight of her heart. *'What?'*

'Just because you've finally deigned to say sorry doesn't make me ready to accept it.' Or act like all that was needed was a carelessly given, barely meant apology. She wanted more than that. She deserved more than that.

Except, of course, Angelo had nothing more to give. And whether or not he said sorry for the past made no real difference to either of their futures. *Why* had he brought her up here? Looking at him now, his face taut with annoyance or maybe even anger, Lucia thought she could hazard a guess.

She was no more than an item to be ticked off on his to-do list. Come back to Sicily, buy a hotel, deal with Lucia. Get any messy emotional business out of the way so he could move on to more important things. She supposed she should be grateful she'd warranted any consideration at all.

She took a deep breath. 'So you've said it, Angelo, you've ticked me off your list, and you can go on happily now with your big business deals and fancy living. And I can get back to work.'

And stop acting out this charade that she didn't care, that she'd only been angry or even annoyed. She couldn't understand how Angelo could believe it, yet he obviously did, for he was annoyed too, by her stubbornness. He still had no idea how much he'd hurt her.

'It's been seven years, Lucia,' he said, an edge to his voice, and she met his gaze as evenly as she could.

'Exactly.'

'I haven't even been in Sicily since that night.'

'Like I said before, there's the phone. Email. We live in the twenty-first century, Angelo. If you'd wanted to be in touch, I think you just might have found a way.' He bunched his jaw and she shook her head. 'Don't make excuses. I don't need them. I know that one night was exactly that to you—one night. I'm not delusional.' *Not any more.*

'So you didn't even expect me to call? Or write?'

'No, I didn't.' Even though part of her had stubbornly, stupidly hoped. 'But expecting and wanting are two different things.'

He stared at her for a long, hard moment. 'What did you want?' he asked quietly, and Lucia didn't answer. She would not articulate all the things she had wanted, had hoped for despite the odds, the *obviousness* of Angelo's abandonment. She would not give Angelo the satisfaction of knowing, and so she lifted one shoulder in something like a shrug. 'A goodbye would have been something.'

'That's all? A farewell?'

'I said it would have been *something*.' She tore her gaze from his, forced all that emotion down so it caught in her chest, a pressure so intense it felt like all her breath was being sucked from her body. 'It's irrelevant any-

way,' she continued, each word so very painful to say.
'If you brought me up here to say sorry, then you've said
it. Thank you for that much, at least.'

'But you don't accept my apology,' Angelo observed.
His gaze swept her from head to foot like a laser, searching her, revealing her.

She closed her eyes briefly, tried to summon strength.
'Does it really matter?'

His gaze narrowed, his lips compressed. 'Why do
you ask that?'

'Because you've managed to go seven years without saying sorry or speaking to me at all, Angelo. How
can I help but think my opinions—my feelings—matter
very little to you?' He frowned and she shook her head.
'I'm not accusing you. I'm not angry about it any more.'

'You still seem angry.'

Seem, Lucia thought, being the operative word. If only
it was as simple as that; if only she felt angry that he'd
been so thoughtless as to leave her bed without a word.
If only she felt clean, strong anger instead of this endless
ache of grief. 'I suppose seeing you again has brought it
back, a bit, that's all,' she finally said. She couldn't meet
his gaze. 'Why do you care anyway?'

'I suppose…the same.' Angelo sounded guarded.
'Seeing you again has made me…want to make amends.'

Make amends? As if a two-word reluctant redress
made up for years of emptiness, heartache, *agony*? Did
he really think that was an equal exchange?

But he didn't know. He couldn't know how much she'd
endured, the gossip and shame, the loss and heartbreak.
He had no idea of the hell she'd been through, and she
wouldn't weaken and shame herself by telling him now.

'Well, then,' she said, and her voice sounded flat, lifeless. 'I suppose that's all there is to say.'

Angelo nodded, the movement no more than a terse jerk of his head. 'I suppose so.'

She made herself look at him then, for surely this was goodbye. The goodbye they'd never had. They lived in different worlds now; she was a maid, he was a billionaire. And while she cherished the memory of who he'd once been, she knew she didn't even recognise this haughty man with his hostile gaze and designer suit. He was so different from the tousle-haired boy with the sad eyes and the sudden smile, the boy who had hated her to see him vulnerable and yet had sought her out in the sweetest, most unexpected moments. What had happened to that boy?

Staring at Angelo's hard countenance, Lucia knew he was long gone. And the unyielding man in front of her was no more than a wealthy stranger. She felt a sudden sweep of sorrow at the thought, too overwhelming to ignore, and she closed her eyes. *She missed that boy.* She missed the girl she'd been with him, full of irrepressible hope and happiness. The girl and boy they'd been were gone now, changed forever by circumstance and suffering.

She opened her eyes to see Angelo staring at her, a crease between his brows, a frown compressing his mouth. He had a beautiful mouth, full, sculpted lips that had felt so amazingly soft against hers. Ridiculous that she would recall the feel of them now.

'So may I go?' she asked when the silence between them had stretched on for several minutes. 'Or is there anything else you'd like to say? You might as well say it now, because if you summon me to your office twice the gossip will really start flying.'

Angelo's frown deepened into a near scowl. 'Gossip?'

Lucia just shook her head. She shouldn't have said

that. Angelo didn't know how difficult those months after he'd left had been for her, how in their stifling village community she'd been labelled another Corretti whore...just like his mother had. She didn't want him to know. 'It looks a little suspicious, that's all. Most maids never see the CEO's office.'

'I see.' He paused, glanced down at some papers that lay scattered across his desk. 'I'm sorry. I didn't mean to make things difficult for you.'

'Never mind. May I go now?'

Angelo stared at her for a long moment, and she saw that glimpse of bleakness in his eyes again, and that ache inside her opened right up, consumed her with sudden, desperate need. She wanted to take him in her arms and smooth away the crease that furrowed his forehead. She wanted to kiss him and tell him none of it mattered, because she loved him. She'd always loved him.

Pathetic. Stupid. What kind of woman loved a man who had treated her the way Angelo had treated her?

Her mother, for one. And look how *she* had ended up.

'Yes,' Angelo finally said, and he sounded distant, distracted. He was probably already thinking of his next business deal. He turned away, to face the window. 'Yes, of course you can go.'

And so she did, slipping silently through the heavy oak doors even as that ache inside her opened up so she felt as if she had nothing left, *was* nothing but need and emptiness. She walked quickly past the receptionist and felt tears sting her eyes.

Alone in the lift she pressed her fists against her eyes and willed it all back, all down. She would not cry. She would not cry for Angelo Corretti, who had broken her heart too many times already so she'd had to keep fitting it back together, jagged pieces that no longer made a healthy whole. Still she'd done it; she'd thought she'd succeeded.

Alone in the lift with the tears starting in her eyes and threatening to slip down her cheeks, she knew she hadn't.

Angelo stared blindly out the window, his mind spinning with what Lucia had said. And what she hadn't said.

His first reaction had been, predictably, affront. Anger, even. What kind of person didn't accept an apology? He'd had no need to call her up here. He could have ignored her completely.

Yet even as he felt anger flare he'd known it was unreasonable. Unjust. He'd treated her badly, *very* badly considering their childhood friendship, their history. He'd always known that even if he tried not to think of it. Tried not to remember that one tender night.

Seeing her last night had raked up all those old memories and feelings, and he knew he couldn't be distracted from his purpose here. So she'd been right; his apology had been, in a sense, an item on his to-do list.

Deal with Lucia and then move on.

Except as he stood there and silently fumed, staring out the window without taking in the view, he knew he wasn't moving on at all. Seeing Lucia had mired him right back in the past, remembering how he'd been with her. Who he'd been. She'd seen him at his most vulnerable and needy, at his most shaming and pathetic. The thought made his fists clench.

He'd hoped apologising to Lucia would give them both a sense of closure, but he didn't think it had. At least for him it had only stirred things up even more.

Gazing blindly out the window, he saw the bright blue of her eyes, the determined tilt of her chin. When had she become so strong, so *hard*? He'd thought, he realised now, that she'd be glad of his apology, grateful for his attention. He'd expected her to trip over herself accepting his grudging *sorry*.

Instead she'd seemed…indifferent. Uncaring. *Hard*.

He spun away from the window.

He hated this feeling of restless dissatisfaction that gnawed at him, ate away any sense of achievement he'd had over his recent business successes. He hated the raw emotion he felt about Lucia, an uncomfortable mix of guilt and vulnerability and need. Why couldn't he just forget about her? Regardless of whether she had accepted his apology or not, at least he'd given it. The matter was done. It should have been, at any rate.

He sat down at the desk, pulled a sheaf of papers towards him, determined not to think of her again. He'd managed not to think of her for seven years; surely an hour or two wouldn't be difficult.

Yet the minutes ticked by and Angelo just sat there, staring at the papers in front of him without taking in a single word.

CHAPTER THREE

'FRESH TOWELS ARE needed in the penthouse suite.'

Lucia glanced up from where she'd been stacking laundered linens in one of the supply cupboards.

'The penthouse suite?' she repeated, and felt dread— as well as a betraying anticipation—sweep through her. 'Can't someone else go?' She'd been avoiding the penthouse suite or any of the hotel's public places since her confrontation with Angelo.

She'd seen the speculative, sideways glances when she'd walked out of his office, had heard the whispers fall to a hush when she'd entered the break room. She knew people were wondering, some of them remembering, and she couldn't stand the thought of any more speculation or shame. She also couldn't stand the thought of seeing Angelo again, knowing he would look at her as if she were no more than an irritating problem he had to solve. She didn't have the strength to act indifferent, uncaring. He'd see through her thin facade at some point, and she could bear that least of all.

'Signor Corretti asked for you in particular,' Emilia, one of the other chambermaids, returned with a smirk. 'I wonder what he wants besides the towels?'

Lucia stilled. She knew Emilia from her childhood, knew the other woman had never liked her—had in fact seemed jealous of her, which was ridiculous considering how lonely her life had been since Angelo's sudden departure. Emilia would certainly relish any gossip Angelo's personal requests stirred up now. Swallowing, she nodded.

'Fine.' And she'd tell Angelo to leave her alone while she was at it. She took a deep breath and reached for several of the velvety soft towels. If Angelo owned the hotel, she'd have to see him again at some point. The more she got used to it, the less it would hurt. She hoped.

Still Lucia couldn't keep the dread from pooling like acid in her stomach as she headed up the service lift to the top floor, the towels clutched to her chest. Maybe he wouldn't be there. Maybe he'd put in the request for towels and then gone out…*somewhere*…

Except of course that was ridiculous, if he'd made the request himself. He obviously wanted to see her, was summoning her like a—

No. She wouldn't think that way.

The lift doors opened directly into the suite, and Lucia took a step into the silent foyer. She couldn't see or hear Angelo anywhere.

She glanced cautiously towards the living area before she decided to just head for the bathroom, deposit the towels and get out of there as quickly as possible. Taking a deep breath, she hurried down the hall and had her hand on the doorknob of the bathroom when the door swung open and Angelo stood there, dressed only in a pair of dress slacks, his chest bare, droplets of water clinging to his golden skin.

Lucia stood as if rooted to the spot, the towels clutched to her chest, every thought evaporating from her brain. Finally she moistened her lips and managed, 'You wanted towels—'

'Towels?' He frowned, glancing at the towels still clutched against her chest. 'I didn't ask for any towels.'

Lucia felt colour rush to her face. 'You—you didn't?' Which meant Emilia had been mistaken—or lying. Had the other maid set her up for more gossip? Now she could whisper to everyone how Lucia had sneaked up to the penthouse suite late at night? Lucia knew what it would look like. And from Angelo's narrowed gaze, she had a feeling he knew what it looked like too.

Angelo gazed at Lucia, her cheeks touched with colour but her eyes still frustratingly blank. Once he'd been able to see so much clear emotion in those blue, blue eyes of hers. He'd read her so easily because she'd never tried to hide what she felt. How much she felt. He'd taken for granted, he saw now, the hero-worship she'd had for him when they were children. He'd always known it wasn't real, couldn't be, and yet he missed it. He missed, if not the childish adoration she'd once had for him, then at least the affection. The regard.

She looked now as if she didn't care for him at all. As if he were a stranger of no importance. Anger or even hatred would have been easier to accept. It would have been understandable.

But this cold indifference in her eyes—it chilled him. Reminded him of Carlo Corretti's uncaring stare when he'd confronted the man who had fathered him with the hard truth of his identity.

All you were meant to be was a stain on the sheets.

He couldn't stand for Lucia to look at him that way, as if he didn't matter. Didn't exist.

'I didn't order any towels,' he said again, wondering if she had possibly used it as an excuse to see him.

But no—she looked like she'd rather be anywhere else. With anyone else.

'It must have been a mistake,' Lucia said stiffly. 'I'll go.'

She turned and started down the hall, and some insane impulse had Angelo springing forward, reaching for her wrist. 'No—'

She stilled, his fingers still wrapped around her wrist. 'Angelo,' she said in a low voice. 'Don't.'

He could feel the pulse in her wrist hammering hard, and it gratified him. Underneath that cold indifference she felt something. Just as he did. 'Don't what?' he asked softly.

'Don't do this,' she said helplessly. 'What happened between us is over. I know that. It's fine.'

'It is not fine.'

She turned back to him, genuine confusion clouding her eyes to a stormy grey. '*Why?* Why do you ever care what I think or feel?'

'Because—' He heard his voice rise in frustration. *Because I can't stop thinking about you. Because when I finally fall asleep at night I dream of your eyes, your mouth, your softness.* What would it take to stop thinking about this woman? To get her out of his head completely?

Lucia's gaze swept over him and then she angled her head away, hiding her face. Her eyes. 'I must go.' She turned towards the lift, extended one hand towards the button.

Without thinking about what he was doing Angelo lunged forward, trapped her hand with his against the panel of buttons. 'Don't.'

She stilled, and he realised how close he was to her, his body pressing hers against the wall next to the lift. He could feel the heat coming off her lithe, athletic frame, and also the awareness. It coiled and snapped between them like a live wire, an attraction he'd felt—and surrendered to—all those years before. An attraction he still felt now—and with a thrill of satisfaction he knew she felt it too. It *wasn't* over.

He lowered his head so his lips brushed the dark softness of her hair, inhaled the clean, warm scent of her.

'Lucia,' he murmured, and he felt her tense even more.

'Let me go, Angelo.' Her voice trembled and broke on the note of his name and he felt a savage surge of triumph at knowing how affected she was. How attracted.

His lips brushed her hair again and with one hand he drew her own away from the lift button. A shudder wracked her body at his touch, and Angelo felt another thrill surge through him at her blatant response.

He laced his fingers with her own and put his other hand on her shoulder, gently turning her around so her back was against the lift, her body towards him.

He pressed against her and although she remained tense he could still feel her response, her body arching helplessly towards his. This was what he'd wanted all along, he acknowledged with a sudden, primal certainty. This was what he couldn't forget. What he wouldn't forget.

And this was how he would finally exorcise himself of her.

She'd lowered her head, her hair sliding in front of her face. He tucked a tendril behind her ear.

'Don't—' she whispered, but the single word ended on a shudder of longing.

'Don't what?' Angelo asked huskily. 'Don't touch you, or don't stop?' He trailed his fingers down her cheek, let his thumb caress the intoxicating fullness of her lips. Another shudder, and he felt the answering ache inside him. She was so soft. Lips, hair, the curve of her cheek. 'Don't kiss you?' he murmured, and then he did.

Her lips were as sweet and warm as he remembered, and after only a second's pause they parted beneath his own. He swept his tongue into her mouth's softness, his hands sliding from her shoulders to her waist and then to her hips, pulling her closer to him, fitting her against his arousal.

Her hands came up to his shoulders, her fingers curling around as she responded to his kiss, her tongue meeting his, her mouth and body accepting him as they had before.

Triumph and something far deeper and needier surged through him. How had he ever lived without this? Without *her*?

He moved his hand upwards to cup the warm swell of her breast, felt her shuddering response. Then he felt a tear splash onto his cheek and he jerked away as if that single drop had scorched him.

'*Maledizione*, you're crying?'

Lucia dashed the tear from her face. 'You think I want this?' she snapped, her voice choked and yet still filled with furious pride. 'You think I want a repeat of what happened before? Another one-night stand?'

'I...' At a loss, Angelo just shook his head. He'd thought her so hard, so indifferent, yet in that moment it seemed no more than a charade. She couldn't hide the honest emotion in her eyes, and it was despair. *Grief.* 'Lucia...'

'Don't.' Her voice came out clogged and she shook her head. 'Please don't, Angelo.' She turned from him, her whole body trembling, and pressed the button for the lift.

She didn't say anything else and neither did he as they waited for the lift doors to open. He was still reel-ing from shock at the naked sorrow that had swamped her eyes when the doors opened and she stepped inside. She didn't turn around to face him and Angelo felt that familiar pressure build in his chest, throb in his temples. He didn't want her to go. Not like this—

The doors closed on both of their silence.

He stood there for a moment, his head aching, his heart aching. Damn his heart. Damn *hers*. Why had she looked so sad? So lost? He'd thought she was strong, hard. Indifferent…yet she hadn't been indifferent to him in his arms. He'd thought then she felt the same consuming desire and need he felt, not sadness. Grief.

When he'd gazed down at her she'd looked…*broken*.

He didn't want to think about why.

He turned from the lift and stalked over to his laptop, pulling it resolutely towards him, determined to forget about Lucia once and for all.

He couldn't be distracted from his purpose here. He had work to do, more deals to make, more plans to put into motion. Battaglia wanted to meet him and discuss the docklands regeneration project. Luca's fashion business could be ripe for a hostile takeover. Even Gio and his horses on the other side of the island might show a weakness. The Corretti empire was surely starting to crumble, and he'd be the one to sweep up the pieces.

He was on the cusp, Angelo reminded himself, of having everything he'd ever wanted.

So why now, as ever, did he feel so empty?

CHAPTER FOUR

LUCIA'S LEGS TREMBLED and she sagged against the side of the lift as it plunged downwards, away from Angelo. She could still feel the taste of him on her lips, the strong press of his hard body against hers. Even now desire flowed through her in a molten river, making her sag even more against the wall. Making her even weaker.

For she was weak, so pathetically weak, to still respond to him. To still want him, even though she knew he would never think of her as anything more than—*what?*

Why had he kissed her? The answer, the only possible answer, was glaringly apparent. Because he knew he could have her—and then walk away. Because he knew that just as before she would take him in her arms, into her body, and then he could leave without so much as an explanation. She was the easy option, just as her mother had been, accepting a man who treated her like dirt. Wanting him, even begging him, back.

She had never wanted to be like that. She still didn't. She *wouldn't*.

Lucia closed her eyes, forced back the sting of tears. Forced back all the emotion, all the useless regret and anger and hurt. At least she'd shown him she was different now…if only just. At least this time she'd been the one to walk away. If only just.

Two hours later, her heart and body aching, she climbed the steps to the tiny apartment she rented over a bar in Caltarione, the small village near the Correttis' palazzo. She's grown up in a tiny, terraced house farther down the main street, next to Angelo and his grandparents. She'd thought of leaving the village after Angelo had gone, after she'd endured the bold stares and muttered curses that had accompanied her wherever she went for months after his departure, but she hadn't.

Perhaps it was stubbornness or maybe just sentimentality, but she wasn't willing to leave the only place she'd considered home. She wouldn't be driven out, even if the busy streets of Palermo might offer more anonymity and acceptance.

In any case, the whispers and rumours and sneers had died down in the years since Angelo had left. They'd returned, a little, with him; she recognised the speculative looks Emilia and some of the other housekeeping staff who knew her history had given her in the past week. But she ignored it all, with a determination that had sapped all of her strength.

She certainly didn't feel like she had any left now. Resisting Angelo had taken everything.

Kicking open the door to her apartment Lucia discarded her sensible shoes and stripped the soiled maid's uniform from her body. She headed towards the tiny bathroom in the back of the flat and turned the taps on the small, rather dingy tub. She sank onto the edge of the bath and dropped her head in her hands. She felt so unbearably, achingly tired, tired of pretending all the time that she was strong, that she barely cared or remembered about what happened seven years ago. Why had she insisted on this ridiculous charade of indifference? Was it simply out of pride?

But no, she knew it was not as simple a matter as that. She knew this charade was as much for her own benefit as Angelo's. Some absurd part of her believed, or at least hoped, that if she acted like she didn't care, she wouldn't. If she told him it didn't matter, it wouldn't.

And yet it did matter. So very much. It had mattered then, and it mattered now. And while she'd convinced herself that he didn't need to know the truth, maybe she needed him to.

The thought was both novel and frightening. She didn't want to tell Angelo the truth of their night together, and yet as long as she kept it a secret it festered unhealed inside her soul. What if she lanced that wound, drained it of its poison and power? What if she told Angelo, not for his sake, but for her own?

Would she finally be able to put the whole episode behind her, put Angelo behind her?

If only.

She stayed in the tub until the water had grown cold and then she slipped on a pair of worn trackie bottoms and a T-shirt. After a second's pause she took an old cardboard box from the dusty top shelf of her wardrobe, brought it out to the sofa in the living room. She didn't take this box out very often; it felt like picking off the scab of her barely healed soul. She knew it was dangerous weakness to take it out now, when she already felt so raw, yet still she did it, unable to resist remembering.

Carefully she eased the lid off the box and looked at the few treasures inside: a scrapbook of old travel postcards she'd been given from the people whose houses she and her mother had cleaned. She and Angelo had used to make up stories about all the different places they'd travel to one day, the amazing things they would do. A single letter Angelo had written her from New York, when he'd left at eighteen years old. She'd practically memorised its few lines. A lock of hair.

She took the last out now, fingering its silky softness, a tiny curl tied with a bit of thread. She closed her eyes and a single tear tracked down her cheek. It hurt so much to remember, to access that hidden grief she knew she would always carry with her, a leaden weight inside her that never lightened; she had simply learned to limp along under its heaviness.

A sudden, hard rapping on the front door made her still, tense. The only person who ever knocked on her door was the owner of the bar downstairs, an oily man with a sagging paunch who was always making veiled—and not-so-veiled—references to what he thought he knew of her past. She really didn't feel like dealing with him now.

Another knock sounded, this one even more sharp and insistent.

Drawing a deep breath, Lucia put the box and its contents aside. She wiped the tear from her face and looked through the fogged eyehole in the door, shock slicing straight through her when she saw who it was. No oily landlord, and definitely no paunch.

Angelo raised his hand to knock again and, her own hands shaking, she unlocked the door and opened it.

'What are you doing here, Angelo?'

His hair was rumpled like he'd driven his fingers carelessly through it, his expression as grim as ever. 'May I come in?'

She shrugged and moved aside. Angelo stepped across the threshold, his narrowed gaze quickly taking in the small, shabby apartment with her mother's old three-piece suite and a few framed posters for decoration. It wasn't much, Lucia certainly knew that, but it was hers and she'd earned it. She didn't like the way Angelo seemed to sum it up and dismiss it in one judgemental second.

'What do you want?' she asked, and heard how ragged her voice sounded. 'Or do you not even know? Because you keep trying to find me, but God only knows why.'

He turned slowly to face her. 'God only knows,' he agreed quietly. 'Because I don't.'

'Then maybe you should just stop.'

'I can't.'

She shook her head helplessly, every emotion far too close to the surface, to his scrutiny. 'Why not?'

'I...' He stared at her, his eyes glittering, wild. His lips parted, but no sound came out. Lucia folded her arms, conscious now that she was wearing a thin T-shirt and no bra.

'Well?' she managed.

'Back in my hotel suite,' Angelo said slowly. 'At the lift.' His gaze roved over her, searching. 'Why did you look at me like that?'

'Like what?'

'As if...as if you were sad.'

Lucia swallowed. 'Don't, Angelo,' she said, her voice no more than a rasp. 'Please, just leave it.'

'I can't.'

'You *can*. You're like a dog with a bone.' She shook her head, anger warring with the agony as well as the deep-seated desire she had to hide it. 'Just leave me alone.'

'You think I don't want to?' Angelo asked quietly, and she let out a sudden, wild laugh, the unfettered sound surprising them both.

'Oh, I know you want to. You've always wanted to. Everything you've taken from me has been against your better judgement, even your will. You think I don't know that?'

Angelo was silent for a long moment. 'Why do you offer it, then?' he finally asked. 'All the kindnesses when we were children—and before…that night—'

That night. She did not want to remember the hope, the *joy*, that had coursed through her when Angelo had kissed her. When she thought he'd felt just as she did, had built a castle in the air of her dreams, as insubstantial as the mist on the sea, gone by morning, as she'd surely known he would be.

'Because we were friends, Angelo,' she forced out. 'Because, when we were children, I saw the sadness in your eyes and I wanted to wipe it away. I wanted to help you—' *I wanted to love you.* She swallowed down the words.

'I've never wanted *help*.'

'I know that. How could I not know that, when you constantly pushed me away? And yet I kept trying.' She shook her head, forced herself to laugh, as if it was all in the distant, unimportant past. 'I was foolish, as a kid.' And as a woman.

'And that night?' Angelo asked in a low voice. 'Why did you sleep with me?'

'Isn't it obvious?' She turned around with a shrug, every atom of her being focused on appearing hard, strong. 'I wanted you. I've always been attracted to you.'

'And that was it? A one-night stand, pleasurable for both of us?'

She jerked her head in the semblance of a nod. She couldn't manage anything more.

Angelo shook his head. 'There's more.' He took a step towards her, his mouth a hard line, his gaze seeming to bore right into her. 'If that's the truth, Lucia, you wouldn't have looked like you did back there, by the lift. You wouldn't have looked like I'd broken your heart—'

'You *did* break my heart.' The words exploded from her like a gunshot, a crack in the taut silence of the room. She saw shock flash in Angelo's eyes and she turned away quickly.

'Then—'

'It's not what you think.' She drew in a ragged breath. Now was the time for truth, or at least part of it. She still couldn't tell him how much she'd loved him, admit all that weakness, but she could tell him about the consequences of their one night. Perhaps he'd already guessed it; perhaps that was why he kept at her, asking questions, demanding answers. He knew she was hiding something.

'What do I think, Lucia?' Angelo asked quietly.

She shook her head, her back still to him. 'It doesn't matter what you think.'

'No?'

'You don't *know*, Angelo.' She dragged in a breath, the very air hard to breathe, heavy inside her. 'You don't understand—'

'Then tell me.' He came to stand behind her, one hand hard on her shoulder. 'Tell me what I don't know.'

Lucia closed her eyes, tried to find the words. She hadn't been able to find them in all the letters she'd written and never sent, and she searched uselessly for them now. She licked her lips. 'That night…'

'Yes?' Angelo prompted, impatient now, his fingers digging into her shoulder.

'There were…consequences….'

'Consequences?' Angelo's voice sharpened and she couldn't answer. 'Look at me, damn it.' With his hand on her shoulder he turned her around, forced her to face him. 'What have you been keeping from me?' he demanded, and she saw the anger in his eyes, but worse, far worse, she saw the fear. She felt it.

He knew. Maybe he didn't realise he knew, but he knew.

'I was pregnant, Angelo,' she whispered. 'I had a baby.'

CHAPTER FIVE

ANGELO DROPPED HIS hands from her shoulders and stared at her utterly without expression, his body completely still. Lucia had no idea what he was thinking or feeling. Maybe it was nothing. Maybe he didn't even care. He certainly wouldn't grieve their daughter the way she had. He might not even believe her.

His gaze moved over her slowly, as if searching for answers, for weaknesses. 'Are you saying,' he asked in a voice devoid of expression, 'that you became pregnant, after that night? That one time?' She nodded. 'You had a baby? A child?' She nodded again, the words to explain stuck in her throat, jagged shards of memory and loss that cut open everything inside her. He continued to stare at her, hard, first in assessment, and then in acceptance.

She saw the emotions move over his face: first the shock, followed by a flash of anger, and then an under-standing. And finally, the most unexpected emotion of all, an eager hope softening his features as his mouth half quirked into an incredulous, tremulous smile. 'A boy,' he asked hoarsely, 'or a girl?'

Lucia closed her eyes against the agonising emotion so apparent on his face. She'd steeled herself for anger, accusations, maybe even disbelief. But hope? *Happiness?* They hurt so much more. 'A girl,' she whispered.

'But where—where is she?' She opened her eyes and saw Angelo looking around as if he expected a bright-eyed, curly-haired six-year-old to come bounding up to him with a smile. 'What is her name?'

'Angelica,' Lucia whispered, the word tearing her throat, hurting her.

'Angelica...' She saw a smile dawn across Angelo's face then disappear. His eyes narrowed, the hope fading from them. 'Where is she, Lucia?'

She just shook her head, unable to speak, to tell him. 'Where is she?' he demanded, urgent now, rough. He took her by the shoulders again, stared at her hard, and through the mist of her own tears she saw the bleakness in his eyes, and she knew just as before he already knew.

'She's dead.'

She felt Angelo's fingers clench on her shoulders before he released her and turned away. Neither of them spoke and Lucia drew a ragged breath into her lungs.

'How?' he finally asked tonelessly.

'She—she was stillborn. At seven months. The cord was wrapped around her neck.' She drew another breath, just as ragged. 'She was perfect, Angelo.'

Angelo shook his head and made some small sound, his back to her, and she had the sudden urge to comfort him, just as she had many times before. Take him in her arms, draw his head to her shoulder. This time she didn't move. It was too late for that. Far, far too late.

Slowly he turned back around, his face now wiped of any emotion or expression at all. Lucia remained still, everything in her aching. She wanted him to say something, *do* something, but he didn't move or speak.

After an endless moment his gaze fell on the box of treasures she'd left on the sofa. Lucia made one involuntary move towards it, as if she could hide the evidence of her sentimentality. Angelo's letter, the scrapbook they'd once pored over...

The lock of hair.

His gaze remained steadfastly on that little curl of sadness and then he lifted it to hers. 'May I?' he asked, and wordlessly she nodded.

She watched as Angelo took the silky bit of baby hair in his hand and ran its softness between his fingers. He didn't say anything, and his head was lowered so Lucia couldn't see his face.

'Angelo...' she whispered, although she had no idea what she would say. That she'd never forgotten him? That she'd held their daughter in her arms and grieved not just her precious child but the life she'd thought, for one blissful night, could be hers? That she'd loved him?

And loved him still.

Carefully Angelo returned the lock of the hair to the box. Lucia saw his gaze flick over the other items, but she couldn't tell if he recognised the scrapbook or letter. Then he looked directly at her, and she could see nothing in his grey-green gaze. It was as hard and unyielding as it had ever been.

'I should go.'

Disappointment and even despair flooded her, but somehow she managed to nod again. She didn't trust herself to speak, didn't know what she would say. He nodded back, in farewell, and then she watched as he strode towards the door and out into the night. Once again he'd left her alone and aching, just as he had before.

Angelo didn't remember much about the drive back to the hotel. His mind was a blur of memories and thoughts he could not articulate. He kept his gaze focused on the road, but he didn't even remember driving.

He pulled up to the hotel and tossed the keys to a valet, then strode through the lobby, blind to everyone and everything around him. He rode up the lift up to the penthouse suite and strode through the empty, ornate rooms before ending up in the bathroom, staring at his pale, wild-eyed reflection.

Then he clenched his hand into a fist and punched that reflection as hard as he could. Glass shattered in an explosion of glittering fragments and blood welled up on his knuckles, trickled down his wrist.

Angelo swore and reached for one of the towels—one that Lucia had brought—and pressed it to his bloody fist. What an idiotic, uncontrolled thing to do. Yet even with his hand throbbing he couldn't regret it. He'd needed some outlet for his rage. His agony.

It was sudden, this grief that overwhelmed him, sudden and utterly unexpected. He'd never felt it before, and yet it was also weirdly familiar. He felt as if he'd been feeling it all his life, suppressing it, hiding it—even from himself.

He hadn't grieved his mother when she'd left him at six years old, with a careless kiss and a guilty look. He'd seen her again once, when he was thirteen and she'd come home asking for money.

He hadn't grieved the death of his grandparents, who had taken care of him for his entire childhood and died within a few months of each other when he was eighteen. They hadn't loved him, he knew that. They'd been ashamed of him, the Corretti bastard nobody had wanted.

He hadn't even grieved the father he'd never had, the man who had told him, point blank, he'd have preferred for Angelo not to exist at all. And even when Carlo Corretti had died, Angelo had felt…nothing. He'd always felt nothing.

Until now. Now when that surface nothing cracked like the thinnest ice and revealed the depth and darkness of the emotion churning below. Raw, honest, messy grief rose up inside him, threatened to spill out. His eyes stung and his throat thickened with tears and over what? A baby he'd never expected to have? A life he'd never even thought he wanted?

A daughter. A daughter with silky dark hair and his name. Angelo blinked hard.

With the towel still pressed to his hand he crunched across the broken glass and went back out to the living room, stared unseeingly at the city stretched out before him like a glittering chessboard and he was the king.

That's how he'd seen his life: an arduous journey from pawn to king, strategising and calculating every single move he'd ever made, and all, only to win.

Yet now he felt only loss—unbelievable, unending—flooding through him, filling his emptiness with something far worse. *Grief.*

Slowly he sank onto a sofa, his hand cradled in his lap. He felt as if he were spinning into a void, with no plans, no thoughts. He had no idea what to do now.

Forge ahead, forget what was behind? Forget this daughter he'd never known, and the woman who had been her mother, who might have been his wife?

Could he forget Lucia?

It was a question he'd never asked himself before. He'd never even thought to ask it; forgetting her had been a given. But now…now he wasn't so sure.

Now, Angelo thought bleakly, he wasn't sure of anything.

He closed his eyes, fought against all that emotion surging within him, rising up. Why hadn't she told him about the baby? And if she had, what would he have done? Could he have changed the awful course of events?

He knew, rationally, that he couldn't have, and yet still he wondered. Wished even, for a life he'd never thought to have. And as for the future... He knew there was still something between him and Lucia. Whether it was no more than the remnant of a childhood affection that had long since eroded into antipathy or something more, something good he didn't know. But he intended to find out.

How?

Clearly Lucia wanted him to leave her alone. To forget. And in some ways, it would be easier to forget. To go on as he always had before.

And yet he knew he couldn't. Wouldn't. Grimly Angelo stared straight ahead, his bleeding, throbbing hand momentarily forgotten. He wasn't done here. *They* weren't done...no matter what Lucia wanted or thought.

Lucia woke with her eyes feeling gritty and her mouth dry as dust. She'd barely slept, having spent most of the night trying to blank out the memories that kept looping in a relentless reel through her mind. The doctor's flat voice telling her Angelica was dead. The softness of her daughter's still-warm skin when she'd held her. The blank look on Angelo's face last night.

She'd thought—for a single moment, she'd *believed*— that he cared about Angelica, if not about her. She'd thought, when his back had been turned, he'd been grappling with grief but when he'd turned around again he had looked only blank, as if he'd accepted and absorbed the news in the space of a few minutes, and was now moving on.

Always moving on.

She needed to move on too, Lucia knew, in so many ways. She showered and dressed, plaited her hair and drank a cup of strong coffee. She'd thought she had moved on years ago, had told herself she had. She'd stopped thinking about Angelo, had tried to remember only the good things about their time together as children. She'd thought she'd accepted Angelica's death, had even told herself that it could be better this way. She hadn't really had the resources to care for a child, a baby who would be labelled another Corretti bastard from the moment she'd taken her first breath.

A breath she'd never been able to take.

Firmly Lucia pushed all these thoughts out of her mind. She was done with this. Done with grief, with sorrow, with Angelo. She wished he'd never returned to rake up all these feelings inside her, even as she acknowledged with stark honesty that she was still—*still*—glad he had returned.

She took the bus into Palermo, watched the dust billow into brown clouds along the road and resolutely did not think of Angelo. Of Angelica. Of any of it.

She worked all morning, cleaning bedrooms on the second and third floors, happy to be occupied with hard work. During her break she chatted with Maria, who proudly showed her a letter her son had written from Naples.

'Will you… Will you read it to me?' she asked hesitantly, for like many of the housekeeping staff Maria was not a fluent reader.

Lucia nodded and took the thin piece of paper. She'd finished with school at sixteen, but she'd studied hard and she liked to read. The letter was short enough, just a few pithy paragraphs describing his rented accommodation, the job he had in a canning factory. Lucia read it aloud before folding it back into the envelope and handing it to Maria.

'He sounds like he's doing well.'

'Yes. Yes.' Maria dabbed at her eyes with the corner of her apron. 'I'm a foolish woman, I know, to carry on so. But he's a good boy. And he did write. That's something, yes?'

'Of course it is,' Lucia told her, but inside she felt leaden. Angelo had written her one letter, just as short and matter-of-fact as Maria's son's, yet she'd treasured it. She'd read it so many times the paper had worn thin in places, and her mother had clucked her tongue and told her not to be stupid, not like she was.

Yet she had been. She'd been so incredibly, utterly stupid about Angelo.

How could she be so again, to think of him? Want him? She'd exhausted herself all morning trying *not* to think of him, a pointless endeavour since her brain and body insisted on remembering everything she'd loved about him. Still did. The silvery green of his eyes, the colour of dew drops on grass. The sudden quirk of his smile, so rare, so precious. The sure feel of his hands on her, reaching for her, *needing* her.

'Do you think he'll write again?' Maria asked, and Lucia blinked, focused on the older woman instead of her agonising thoughts.

Swallowing hard, she smiled at Maria. 'I'm sure he will write.'

Maria nodded and put the letter into the pocket of her apron. 'I'll wait,' she said, and Lucia just nodded, unable to keep herself from thinking, *That's what I did. And even though I don't want to be, I still am.*

By six o'clock she was bone-tired, and outside the air was hot, still and dusty. Her feet throbbed as she walked to the street corner to wait for the bus that would take her back to Caltarione.

Traffic flowed by her in an indifferent stream, cars honking and mopeds weaving around dusty taxi cabs. Lucia was just about to sink onto a bench when a Porsche glided up to the kerb and the window slid down.

'Lucia.'

'What do you want, Angelo?' she asked tiredly.

She couldn't see him very well in the dark interior of the car, no more than the hard line of his cheek and jaw, the silvery-green glint of his eyes. 'I looked for you at the hotel but you'd already gone. I need to speak with you.'

She shook her head. Surely they had no more to say each other. 'About what?'

'About Angelica.' And just like that her assumptions scattered and her throat went tight. 'Please,' he said quietly. 'I need to know.' Wordlessly she rose from the bench and slid into the sumptuous leather interior of the car.

Angelo pulled smoothly away from the kerb and they drove in silence down the boulevard towards Quattro Canti, the historic centre of Palermo, its Baroque buildings now gilded in fading sunlight. Lucia watched the buildings stream by in a blur until they were out of the city, and speeding down a dusty road towards Capaci, the sea shimmering in the distance.

'Where are we going?' she asked after the silence had stretched on for several minutes.

'My villa.'

'Your villa?' She turned to him in surprise. 'Why do you stay at the hotel if you have your own villa nearby?'

Angelo lifted one powerful shoulder in a shrug, his gaze still on the road. 'It's more convenient to stay at the hotel.'

They didn't speak again until Angelo pulled up on

a long, curving drive and parked in front of his villa. The place was sleek and utterly modern, made of local stone and built into the rocky hillside so it seemed to blend with the landscape. Lucia followed him inside and stood in the centre of the soaring living room; the furniture was all chrome and leather, top-of-the-line and completely sterile.

Angelo tossed his keys on a side table and loosened his tie. 'Would you like a shower? Or to change?'

She shrugged, although she would have liked to freshen up. 'I don't have any other clothes.'

'That is not a problem. I had some delivered. They're upstairs in one of the bedrooms.'

Shock had her simply staring for a few seconds. 'Why would you do that, if we're just going to have a conversation?'

Now he shrugged, the twist of his shoulders seeming impatient. 'Why not?'

It wasn't, Lucia thought, much of an answer, but she didn't have the energy to question him and the truth was she would kill for a shower. 'Thank you,' she said, as graciously as she could manage, and headed upstairs.

She found the clothes in one of the bedrooms overlooking the sea, several shopping bags' worth from Palermo's most exclusive boutiques. Pocket change to Angelo, of course, but those few bags contained more clothing than she possessed, and were worth far more than anything she owned.

With a ripple of apprehension she headed into the massive marble en suite and stripped off her maid's uniform. It felt good to wash away a day's dirt, but she couldn't shake the uneasy sense that Angelo wanted more from her than just a conversation.

Twenty minutes later, dressed in the most casual

clothes she'd been able to find, a silk T-shirt in pale blue and a matching swishy skirt that ended just above her knee, she went downstairs to find Angelo.

He had obviously showered too, for his hair was damp and curling on his neck and he had changed from his steel-grey suit to a pair of faded jeans and a worn T-shirt in hunter green.

Lucia stood in the doorway of the kitchen and watched him, her breath catching in her chest at the sight of him, the powerful shoulders encased in snug cotton, the flat stomach and trim hips and powerful thighs. He was as beautiful as a Roman statue, and in so many ways just as remote.

Did she really know this man any more? He'd left Sicily fifteen years ago, and she'd only seen him once in all that time. One unforgettable time.

He glanced up, and his eyes seemed even greener as he gazed at her for one long, taut moment before he nodded towards her clothes.

'They fit.'

'Yes. I didn't think you knew my size.'

'I guessed.' He gestured to some containers on the counter in front of him. 'Are you hungry? I realise you probably haven't eaten.'

She was starving and so she nodded, coming into the kitchen to watch Angelo lift the lids off several foil containers.

'I'm not much of a cook,' he said with the tiniest quirk of a smile, 'so I just ordered from the hotel's kitchens.'

'A perk of being the boss, I suppose,' she said, and although she'd meant to sound light she heard a faint note of bitterness creep into her voice, and she knew Angelo heard it too. He glanced up at her, the expression in his eyes veiled.

'Does that bother you? Me being the boss?'

She shrugged, a twitching of her shoulders. 'Why should it?'

'I don't know.'

'Well, I don't know either.' What an inane, childish conversation they were having. Lucia turned away from the sleek granite worktops and prowled around the open living space. 'Has anyone ever lived here?' She had not yet found a single personal item in the entire place, not a book or a photo or even a stray sock. Nothing to tell her more of the man Angelo was now.

'I've never been here before tonight.'

She glanced back at him, shocked. 'Never? Not even to make sure you liked it?'

'I had it built to my specifications, and I have an assistant who handles interior decorating. She knows my preferences.'

Lucia ignored that little splinter of jealousy that burrowed into her at the thought of some female assistant who knew what he liked. More than she knew, because she wouldn't have guessed that Angelo liked such modern decor. She really didn't know anything about him any more.

So how could she still want him? Love him?

Angelo glanced at her, eyebrows raised. 'What do you think of it?'

'You have a beautiful view,' she said diplomatically, and he let out a short, dry laugh.

'I see.'

'It just seems so…sterile. Cold. There's nothing personal about any of it.'

'And why should there be? As I told you, I've never stepped inside the place until half an hour ago.'

'And will you live here? Eventually?'

'No. I'll never live in Sicily.' The finality of his words and tone silenced her. He ladled some manicotti and swordfish onto two plates. 'Let's eat outside.'

Lucia followed him through the sliding glass doors that led to a wraparound veranda with a stunning view of the sea, the setting sun turning its surface to shimmering gold. The surf crashed far below, sending up plumes of white spray onto the railing.

'This is amazing,' Lucia said, gesturing at the view but meaning to encompass everything: the view, the house, Angelo's life. It was all amazing, and she felt a bittersweet pride at how hard he'd worked and how much he'd accomplished.

How far he'd travelled, so far away from her.

Angelo pulled out her chair and she sat, tensing as he spread a cloth napkin in her lap. His thumbs brushed her thighs and even though he'd barely touched her she still felt an ache of longing spread upwards and take over her whole body.

She tried to ignore it, to force it back, because she knew how dangerous that ache of wanting could be. That ache had deceived her, destroyed her. Made her believe in foolish fairy tales and ridiculous happily-ever-afters, even when she'd known they were absurd. Impossible.

'You wanted to talk about Angelica,' she said, smoothing the napkin over her lap once more. That was why she was here, why she'd agreed to come; he deserved to know about his daughter. So she would tell him, and then she would leave. And then, finally, please God, it would truly be finished between them.

Which was what she wanted, had to want, even if everything in her screamed otherwise.

'Yes.' Angelo sat across from her, his gaze fathomless in the near twilight. He reached for the bottle of wine he'd brought out along with their plates and with an arch of an eyebrow indicated if she'd like him to pour.

Lucia shook her head. 'No, thank you.'

Angelo set the bottle back down and reached for his fork. 'You live alone,' he remarked as he started to eat. She nodded, wary, and took a forkful of swordfish. It was buttery-soft and tender, almost dissolving in her mouth. 'What happened to your mother?' he asked.

Lucia swallowed. 'She died seven years ago.' Two months before he'd shown up at her door.

Something flickered in his eyes, although Lucia couldn't tell what it was. What he felt. 'I'm sorry. How did it happen?'

'A heart attack. It was quick.'

'Sudden too.'

'Yes.'

'So you've been on your own a long time.'

'Yes.' He knew from their childhood that she'd been raised by her mother; her father, worthless drunk that he'd been, had left without a backwards glance when she was eight years old, and her mother had never stopped missing him, never stopped wanting him back. Angelo wasn't the only one who'd had unfortunate parents.

'You've been working for the Correttis since I left,' he observed, his tone neutral, and Lucia toyed with her pasta.

'They pay well.'

'Did you mother leave you any money?'

'What little she had.' She glanced up at him, felt a flash of frustration, maybe even of anger. 'Why are you asking all this, Angelo? What on earth does it matter to you?'

'You matter,' he said flatly. 'You were the mother of my child, Lucia. I want to know what has happened to you.'

She shook her head. 'It doesn't change anything.'

'I still want to know.'

They ate in silence for a moment, and Lucia felt tension tauten inside her. She might have been the mother of Angelo's child, but she wasn't—and never had been—anything else to him. It stung that the only reason he'd sought her out now, had spoken to her again at all, was because he wanted to know about Angelica. And even though part of her was gratified and even glad he wanted to know about their daughter, another part shrank back in desolation that he didn't care about *her*.

Still she yearned. Still her stubborn, stupid heart insisted on wanting, on hoping, even when she knew there was no point. No chance.

'Did you try and tell me?' he asked after a long silence, his tone still neutral. 'When you found out you were pregnant?'

'I tried to try,' she answered quietly. 'I didn't know how to tell you. I didn't want you to feel guilty or like I'd trapped you into something, but—' She hesitated, and his mouth twisted.

'But you were afraid I wouldn't believe you? Or come back for you?'

She lifted her chin and made herself meet his hooded gaze directly. 'Would you have?'

'For my child? Yes.' He spoke with complete certainty, and Lucia nodded slowly. For his child. Not for her, never for her. She'd never been enough of a reason for him to stay, or even to consider taking her with him. It was that realisation, she knew, that had kept her from writing. She had never wanted to be his burden.

'In any case,' she said, trying to sound matter-of-fact, 'I wrote a dozen different letters and never sent them. I kept telling myself I had time, and then—and then it didn't matter any more.' She swallowed past the lump that had formed in her throat. Even now it hurt. Especially now.

'I wish,' Angelo said quietly, 'I could have been there. I would have liked to have seen her, to have held her.'

Lucia stared down at her plate, her half-eaten meal blurring in front of her. She knew if she blinked the tears would fall, and she didn't want to cry. Not in front of Angelo. Not when every word he said seemed to hurt her in so many different ways.

He wanted to have been there for their baby, not for her. And even though that knowledge hurt, a far worse pain lanced through her at how easily she could imagine him cradling their daughter, loving her. How much of her still yearned for a life that had never been hers— or theirs.

'She looked just like she was asleep,' she said, her eyes still on her plate. She cleared her throat, the sound unnaturally loud in the sudden stillness. 'I held her for a little while.' She blinked, touched the corner of her eye where a telling moisture had appeared, averting her face so Angelo wouldn't see.

Still she didn't think she'd fooled him.

'Let's walk,' he said, almost roughly, and rose from the table. Lucia looked up, blinking rapidly, and then followed him down the twisting staircase that led to the beach.

CHAPTER SIX

THE WIND OFF the sea was a sultry caress of her skin, the sand soft and still warm under her bare feet. Lucia dabbed at her eyes again, took a deep breath as she wrested her emotions under control. Her composure, her sense of control, was the only thing of value that she had, and she clung to it.

He walked a little ahead of her, his hands shoved into the pockets of his jeans, the wind blowing the T-shirt tight to his body so she could see the powerful, sculpted muscles of his chest and abdomen.

'And afterwards?' he asked after they'd walked for several minutes, the waves washing onto the sand by their feet. 'Was there…was there a funeral?'

'Yes.' She spoke with matter-of-fact flatness, her only defence against the undertow of emotion that threatened to suck her down into its destructive spiral. She hadn't talked of this in so long; she hadn't even allowed herself to remember. Her pregnancy had been a source of shame, so that even her daughter's death had felt like a forbidden grief, not to be spoken of, not to be mourned. More than one woman in the narrow streets of Caltarione had told her she should be thankful Angelica hadn't lived. Lucia had never replied to this repellent sentiment, but everything in her had burned and raged—and now, under the onslaught of Angelo's questions, still did.

'At the church in Caltarione,' she told Angelo in that same matter-of-fact tone. 'It was a very small service.' Just her, the priest and a few friends of her mother who had, to Lucia's surprise, attended with a silent, stolid solidarity. 'She's buried there, in a special area for still-born babies.' She'd used the last of the inheritance from her mother to pay for the headstone.

Angelo nodded, his head lowered, his hands still shoved in his pockets. 'I'd like to go there.' He paused, stopping mid-stride, and reluctantly Lucia turned to him. His gaze moved searchingly over her as he asked, 'Will you go with me?' The request stopped her in her tracks, the grief she'd suppressed for so long like a leaden weight in her chest.

'Lucia?' Angelo prompted, and she couldn't speak, couldn't even shake her head. It was taking all of her strength, all of her will, simply to stand under that oppressive weight, a grief she'd carried with her yet never acknowledged or accepted. Never been able to let go of.

Now it threatened to bury her, and she could not stand the thought of kneeling in front of her baby's grave with Angelo, acknowledging with him the death of their daughter, of all her dreams, the life she'd once hoped to have....

'Lucia.' Angelo took her by the shoulders. 'What is it? What's wrong?'

What was *wrong*? Could he really ask that? Could he really not understand how this was killing her?

She made some small sound, the sound of an animal in pain. Angelo frowned and with the last of her strength Lucia wrenched away from him before he could see the agony on her face. She started running down the beach, back to the villa, anywhere away from him.

She heard Angelo give a muttered curse and then he was coming up behind her, his hands clamping down on her shoulders and turning her towards him. Still she resisted, twisting away from him as the tears streaked down her cheeks and the sobs gathered in her chest, an unbearable pressure finally demanding release.

Angelo wouldn't let her go. His arms came around her, drawing her to him so she was pressed against his chest, his lips on her hair, her face hidden in the warm curve of his shoulder. 'Oh, Lucia…*mi cucciola*…I'm sorry…I didn't realise.… Of course it still hurts. It always hurts.'

The gentleness of his embrace and the tenderness of his words made it impossible for her to fight. Resist. In the safety of his arms she broke, and all the anguish she'd been holding back spilled out of her, so her body shook and tears streamed from her eyes. She couldn't have even said what she was crying for. The loss of her daughter? The loss of Angelo? The loss of everything, all her unspoken hopes, the life she'd so desperately wanted yet had known she would never have.

Angelo drew her down to the sand, his hands stroking her hair as he murmured endearments and words of comfort, his voice low and ragged.

Lucia heard herself saying things and fragments of things she'd never meant to share, hadn't even realised she remembered. 'She had blue eyes, but they were dark. I think they would have been green, like yours.… They wrapped her in a blue blanket and it made me so angry, such a silly thing.… The doctor's hands were so cold and the nurse took her away from me without even asking.…'

And then there were no more words, just sobs tearing

from her chest and coming out of her mouth in ragged gulps as Angelo held and rocked her, offering her the kind of comfort she'd so often given him.

Her face was hidden in the curve of his shoulder, her lips brushing the warm skin just above the collar of his T-shirt, all of it just as he'd once been with her, and acting on instinct and out of need Lucia pressed her lips against his skin in a silent kiss, a mute appeal. She felt Angelo tense, his arms stiffening even as they held her, but she was past caring. Past asking.

The appeal became a demand as she kissed him again, her lips pressing harder against his warm skin. She heard his ragged draw of breath, his arms still around her.

'Lucia…'

But she didn't want words. She wanted this, only this—to take and not to give, to be comforted and not to comfort. Was it wrong? Was it selfish? She didn't care. She needed this. Needed his caress, the only kind of comfort she craved now. She lifted her head from his shoulder and looked at him, but in the twilit darkness she couldn't make out his expression.

She leaned forward and kissed him hard, and his mouth opened under hers even as his hands came up to her shoulders to brace her—or to push her away? She wrapped her arms around him and pressed herself against him. She heard him groan and he deepened the kiss, his tongue sweeping inside and claiming her for his own.

Lucia kissed him back, her hands in his hair and then on his shoulders, sliding beneath his shirt to feel the taut, warm skin underneath. She pushed him back onto the beach and his arms came up around her, their legs tangling together in the sand.

She lay on top of him, shuddered as she felt his hands

slide under her T-shirt, his thumbs brushing across her breasts. She arched into the caress, shifting so she could feel his arousal pressing against her belly. Angelo kissed her, his mouth moving from her lips to her throat, and then the V between her breasts, the pleasure of his touch so intense it felt almost painful, and yet she still wanted more. Needed more.

With one trembling hand she reached down to undo the button on his jeans. Angelo wrapped his fingers around her own, stilling her hand.

'Lucia, no. *Per favore*, not like this.'

'Yes, like this,' she shot back fiercely. 'Exactly like this.'

He shook his head. 'You are sad, grieving—'

'And you were sad and grieving the last time we slept together, Angelo. It helped, didn't it? I helped you forget for a moment.' He stilled, his hand still wrapped around hers, but his grip had slackened and she pushed his hand away, undid his zip. She stroked the hard length of his erection through the silk of his boxers. 'Help me forget,' she whispered. 'Help me forget, even if just for a moment.' She stroked him again, saw him close his eyes, his jaw clenched.

'If you want me to make love to you, I will,' he said raggedly. 'But not here, on the hard sand.'

She let out a wild, trembling laugh. 'Have you become so particular, in the past seven years?' Her creaky, sagging bed had been the setting for their last encounter; he hadn't complained. He hadn't said anything at all.

'Come back to the villa,' he said, and he rose from the sand, buttoning up his jeans before reaching for her hand. Reluctantly Lucia took it. Now that the rawness of the moment had eased she was conscious of how much she'd revealed, from the confessions she'd sobbed out to the tears on her cheeks, and the shameless, desperate way she'd reached for him. Yet even so she still wanted him. Needed what he could give, if just for this one night.

They walked in silence back along the beach, up the stairs to the veranda and then inside to the sterile stillness of the villa. Angelo turned around to face her, his expression watchful, guarded, and Lucia knew he'd suggested they return to the villa not because he had a preference for satin sheets but because he wanted to give her time to change her mind.

Well, she wouldn't. He'd turned to her for comfort and pleasure once; she'd do the same to him. Maybe then it would feel finished between them, a final, equal exchange. Maybe then she could move on.

She lifted her chin. 'Where's the bedroom?'

Surprise flared silver in his eyes and his mouth quirked in a small smile. 'You are constantly amazing me.'

She ignored the warmth that flared through her at his praise. 'Don't patronise me, Angelo.'

'Trust me, I am not. Perhaps tragedy has made you stronger, Lucia, for you have far more spirit now than I ever gave you credit for when we were children.'

'Yes, I do.' Tragedy *had* made her stronger. She was glad he saw it. 'The bedroom,' she prompted, and he smiled faintly even as he watched her, still wary.

'Are you sure about this?'

'Why shouldn't I be?'

'A decision like this should not be made in the heat of the moment—'

'And it's not the heat of the moment right now,' she answered. Still he stared at her, his eyes dark and considering.

'I don't,' he finally said in a low voice, 'want to hurt you.'

Lucia swallowed past the ache his words opened up inside her. He'd hurt so many times in the past, but this time it would be different.

'You won't,' she said. This time she wouldn't let him. She knew what she wanted, what to expect. This time she would be the one to walk away.

It should be simple. He wanted this; clearly, so did she. So why, Angelo wondered, was he not sweeping Lucia up the stairs and into his bed?

Because her tears had been too recent, her grief too raw. Yet he'd turned to her in his own anger and pain; would he not allow her to do the same?

Still he hesitated.

'Don't tell me you have *la gola secca*, Angelo,' she mocked softly. Her eyes glittered sapphire and she walked towards him, determination evident in every taut line of her body, her hips swaying, the silky T-shirt and skirt highlighting the lush curves he'd had his hands on only moments ago.

'No, not a dry throat,' he replied, gazing down at her. 'I'm not afraid.' He just wanted to give her the time to acknowledge *la gola secca* of her own. He didn't want this to be rushed, regrettable. He still didn't know all he wanted from Lucia, but he did know it was more than that.

He tucked a stray tendril of hair behind her ear, trailed his fingers down her cheek. She closed her eyes, drew in a shuddering breath and then opened them to stare straight into his own.

'Make love to me, Angelo. Make love to me, *please*.'

Her broken plea felled him. How could he deny her? How could he resist her? Angelo curled his hands around her shoulders and kissed her softly. At least, it was meant to be a soft kiss, a tender thing, but memory and need crashed over him, reminding him of how accepted he'd felt in her arms, as if her embrace were the only home—the only hope—he'd ever had.

He deepened the kiss, turned it into both a demand and entreaty. His tongue swept into her mouth and he slid his hands under her T-shirt, cupping the lush fullness of her breasts as a sob of longing broke from her throat and she hooked one leg around his, drawing him even closer to her own intoxicating softness.

He'd meant to lead her upstairs, to pull back the satin sheets and lay her down gently, like a treasure. He'd meant to take his time, to make love to her properly, for he knew the last time they'd been together it had been desperate, frantic—and incredible.

And it was just as frantic now—and just as incredible.

Her fingers fumbled with the zip on his jeans and then curled around his erection. He let out a ragged moan as he slid his own hand up the silky length of her thigh and then beneath her underwear straight to the centre of her, his fingers sliding inside her slick warmth even as his brain told him to stop rushing, they had all the time in the world—

Except they didn't. Lucia pulled him closer, arched against him. 'Now, *now*,' she pleaded, her voice almost a sob as she pushed down his jeans and boxers with clumsy, hurried movements. He hoisted her onto the back of the leather sofa, her legs spread wide and open to him. She reached for him, guiding him towards her.

'Lucia…' he muttered, a token protest, for already she was wrapping her legs around his waist, arching against him, and then he was inside her and he let out a ragged gasp of desire because she felt so *good*.

They moved in silent, sweet complicity, and pleasure and something far deeper surged through him, overwhelmed every sense he possessed. He'd thought last time the rightness he'd felt with Lucia had been a product of his own confused grief over his father's death, but he had no such reason this time. No such excuse. The rightness he felt, the completeness, was just as strong, just as powerful—even more so.

This was where he belonged. He, a bastard child rejected by his father and abandoned by his mother, barely tolerated by the grandparents who had raised him and reviled by the villagers who could have been his community, his strength. This—Lucia—was the only place where he felt at home. Where he belonged.

He felt her arch against him and she sobbed out his name, her face buried in his shoulder, as he reached his own climax and drew her even closer to him, never wanting to let her go.

Lucia sagged against Angelo, replete. Tears streaked down her face but they had been good tears, healing tears in their own way. She didn't regret anything. She wouldn't let herself.

He moved, slipping out of her, and she felt an immediate and innate sense of loss. Incredibly, she still wanted him. Gently he tucked her hair behind her ears, wiped the traces of tears from her face. He smiled, his features softened into something almost like tenderness.

'*Dio*, I didn't mean it to be as fast as that.'

She laughed shakily; already this was so different from before. From what she knew. Seven years ago there had been no pillow talk, no exchange at all. Afterwards he'd drawn her to him and she'd curled around his body, silent, singing with an ill-found happiness, and they'd both fallen asleep.

When she'd woken up with the dawn he had already left. She hadn't even been surprised, not really.

'There's nothing wrong with fast.'

'Next time it will be slow.'

Next time? The words, spoken with so much certainty, shocked her. Surely there would be no next time with Angelo.

He tugged on her fingers. 'Come upstairs.'

'Where?'

But he didn't answer, just led her up the winding staircase and then into what was clearly the master bedroom, and then into the huge marble en suite bathroom.

'You're covered in sand. And tears. Let me wash you.'

Wash her? It seemed like an incredibly intimate, tender thing to do, so different from the frantic urgency of what had happened before. This was new, uncertain territory, thrilling and scary. She didn't know this Angelo.... And yet as he led her to the huge glassed-in shower with a wry, tender smile she felt like she'd always know him.

That boy. That girl.

She stood still as Angelo turned on the taps and then slowly stripped the clothes from her body, sliding her skirt down her legs and the T-shirt over her head. Underwear came next, his movements gentle and unhurried, until she was completely naked before him.

She shivered slightly as she stood there; this felt, weirdly, more revealing than what they'd done just moments ago. Angelo swept his gaze over her body and she reacted underneath his considering stare, a splotchy blush appearing across her chest. He laughed softly.

'*Mi cucciola*, are you embarrassed?'

'Yes,' she said, blushing further. She crossed her arms over her breasts. 'You've never actually seen me naked before. And…and don't call me that.'

He frowned before yanking his T-shirt over his head and tossing it to the floor. 'Call you what?'

Lucia was momentarily distracted by the sight of his chest, all hard, golden muscle with a sprinkling of dark hair veeing down to the unbuttoned waistband of his jeans. She swallowed dryly. '*Mi cucciola*. You called me that when we were children.' *My puppy.* Lucia had never known if he'd meant it or not, but her heart had thrilled every time the endearment had slipped so carelessly from his lips. And no matter how tender he seemed now, she knew he'd changed. She had. This was still only, and ever could be, a one-night stand. Another one.

'I'm not that girl any more, Angelo,' she said quietly. 'And you're not that boy.'

Slowly he reached out and wiped the trace of a tear from her cheek with his thumb. 'Am I not?' he asked softly, and she shook her head.

'You know you aren't.'

'I don't know anything any more.' Smiling although his eyes were dark he wrapped his hand around the back of her neck and drew her to him, kissing her gently on the lips. Lucia closed her eyes, felt her heart twist inside her.

She couldn't let him be that boy again. She'd fallen in love with that boy, and he'd broken her heart. She knew he didn't love her, had never loved her, and if she believed in an Angelo that was different from the ruthless and determined tycoon he'd become she'd be lost. Broken. *Again.*

If he really was that boy inside, underneath, she wouldn't be able to walk away after one night. And she had to, for her own sake. One night, on her terms this time, and then in the morning she'd walk away. For ever.

Angelo broke the kiss to gaze at her, a question in his eyes. 'What are you thinking?' he asked softly.

'Nothing.' She swallowed, tried to smile. 'Nothing important.'

He smiled, the curve of his mouth primal and possessive as he led her into the shower. Lucia had never bathed with a man before. She'd never *been* with a man except Angelo, had never had the opportunity or the desire. She'd only wanted Angelo. She'd only loved Angelo.

She had to stop thinking like that.

She watched as Angelo poured some expensive-smelling shower gel onto his hands, smiling at her, his eyes glinting in the dim light.

'What are you—?' she began, but then stopped as he slid his soapy hands over her body and she leaned against the wall as the water streamed over them and Angelo touched her everywhere.

'Two showers in the space of about an hour,' she murmured as a heavy languor crept over her, caused by the sure movements of Angelo's slippery hands. 'I feel *very* clean.'

He laughed softly and slid one hand between her legs. Lucia clutched his wrist. *'Angelo...'*

'I'm *very* thorough,' he said, and as his fingers found her so did his mouth. He kissed her deeply and Lucia clung to his shoulders, pleasure coursing through her at the feel of Angelo's hands, his mouth, everything. She forgot about what she wanted or didn't want, what was safe and what was incredibly dangerous. All she could think, feel, *know*, was his touch.

She let her head rest against his shoulder as he stroked her, bringing her dizzyingly near that precipice of pleasure once more, her body boneless and yet throbbing with need—and then he stopped.

'What—'

'Now my turn.'

'*Your* turn…'

'Touch me, Lucia.'

She heard the ragged plea in his voice and lifted her head from his shoulder, saw him gazing at her with a fierce light in his eyes, turning them almost to emerald. With a thrill she realised she wanted to touch him, touch him in ways she hadn't yet, hadn't dared.

With a tentative smile she reached for the shower gel, pouring some into her palms before she slid her slippery hands over his shoulders, down his chest, across his hips, revelling in the feel of hot skin and hard muscle. Angelo had closed his eyes and he threw his head back as she slid her hand farther down still and curled her fingers around the heavy, hard length of his arousal.

There was nothing rushed or frantic about this, nothing desperate. Every caress was deliberate, and it filled Lucia with a tremulous wonder. Thirty-two years old and she'd had no idea sex could be like this, slow and exploratory and *wonderful*. This wasn't a stolen moment, snatched out of grief or pain; it stretched on, infinite with possibility, with an incredible new intimacy.

But it would end by morning. She had to remember that.

'*Lucia…*' Angelo's voice was a groan as he curled his hands around her shoulders and she stroked him everywhere, delighting in the glorious feel of him.

'*Dio*, I'm not going to last,' he muttered, and then he hoisted her easily, his hands cradling her bottom so her legs came round his hips as he drove inside her. Lucia buried her head in his shoulder but he pulled back, forced her to meet his own glittering gaze.

'Look at me,' he commanded hoarsely as he moved inside her. 'Look at me as I make love to you.'

Lucia obeyed, her gaze riveted on his as their bodies acting in perfect synchronicity, her hips rising up to meet his as he moved inside her. Every protective layer she'd ever had was stripped away in the intense intimacy of his gaze, his body buried inside hers. She couldn't hide from it; she'd been laid utterly, gloriously bare and in that moment she revelled in the exposure.

She felt the pressure and pleasure building inside her, spiralling up and up, and she knew Angelo could see it on her face. Knew he would know when she finally fell.

And he did, kissing her lips as she cried out and her body spasmed around his. Seconds later he found his own shuddering climax and she buried her head in the curve of his neck as the water streamed over them.

Lucia didn't know how long she remained there, cradled against him, her heart pounding hard against his. It could have been a minute or an hour, but eventually Angelo gently righted her, turned off the shower and wrapped her in a towel. She remained still as he dried her tenderly and then led her to the bed.

They didn't speak, and Lucia was glad. She didn't want to break this moment that had wrapped around her like a spell of warmth and safety and love. She knew it wasn't real, knew in the hard light of morning it would all be broken, vanished. But she wasn't ready to let go of it yet.

One night. One night of feeling safe and treasured and loved. It didn't seem too much to ask.

Angelo laid her in the bed and then slid in next to

her, pulling her towards him so she naturally curved her body into his. She could feel his still-pounding heart against her back, and after a moment Angelo found her hand with his own and laced his fingers with hers, resting their joined hands against her belly as sleep finally claimed her.

CHAPTER SEVEN

LUCIA WOKE TO an empty bed. She rolled over on her back, stared at the ceiling and let the memories wash over her. The pleasure of last night, and more surprisingly and poignantly, the incredible intimacy. She hadn't expected that. She'd gone into the evening expecting a bargain, an exchange of both power and pleasure. This time she'd be the one to want the one-night stand. And the one to walk away.

The trouble was, she didn't want to.

She rolled onto her side, tucked her legs up towards her tummy. She was an idiot, of course. An absolute idiot to think she could walk away from Angelo. To think that she could want it. She'd loved him since she was seven years old.

And yet she knew, with a heavy, painful certainty, that walking away was her only choice. Angelo wouldn't want anything else, and she refused to surrender her dignity yet again. This time she would choose first…if he hadn't already.

Slowly she swung her legs over the side of the bed, felt aches in all sorts of places. A glance at the clock told her it was after eight, and she was due at the hotel in less than an hour. She pushed her hair out of her face and went in search of her maid's uniform.

Ten minutes later she was dressed, her hair and teeth brushed thanks to the basket of toiletries in the guest bedroom, and resolutely she went in search of Angelo. She found him in the kitchen, slicing fruit, the tantalising aroma of fresh coffee scenting the air.

Lucia hung back for a moment, watching as he moved around the kitchen. He wore another worn T-shirt, this one in heather grey, and a pair of boxers. His hair was tousled, almost curly in the heat, and he looked comfortable, natural, *happy*. She'd never seen him look so happy before.

And for a second, no more, she let herself imagine that this was real. Lasting. This was their home, their life, a normal morning in a loving relationship. She even, treacherously, allowed herself to imagine their daughter slept upstairs, six years old, with Angelo's eyes and her dimple.

A longing so intense it felt as if she were being suffocated took hold of her, stole her breath. Shakily Lucia drew another, forced the images back.

This was what was real: work in half an hour and whatever little she and Angelo had shared over. Throwing her shoulders back, she came into the kitchen.

Angelo raised his head as soon as he heard her; Lucia saw the welcoming light wink out of his eyes as he stared at her, his mouth compressing into a hard line.

'Why are you wearing that wretched uniform?'

She stiffened at the disdain in his voice. 'Because I'm due at work in less than an hour.'

'Work?' He sounded utterly incredulous. 'I called already. You're not expected.'

'You…called?' Lucia stared at him blankly. Why would he call? Why would he not want her to go to work?

'Yes, I called. Of course you're not going to work today.'

'I'm not?' She prickled, fought against the treacherous surge of hope his words caused to rise up within her. 'Why not?'

His mouth quirked in a smile. 'I think the better question is, why would you?'

'Because it's my job and I don't want to get fired?'

His smile widened. 'Since I now own the hotel I don't think you'll get fired.'

'Don't, Angelo.' Even though she knew he was speaking the truth his words made her cringe. Sleeping with the boss. It sounded so sordid, as sordid as the last time he'd breezed in and out of her life, and left rumours and heartache in his wake.

'Don't what?' He frowned, seeming genuinely confused, and Lucia just shook her head and took a deep breath.

'I think,' she said, 'it would be better—cleaner—if we ended this now.'

Angelo stared at her for a long moment. The frown had gone from his face, just like the smile. He looked utterly unreadable, completely expressionless. 'Cleaner,' he finally said, his tone neutral.

'Yes.'

'You want to end this now?'

'I think it would be better.'

He glanced back down at the melon he'd been slicing and arranged the slices on a plate, his long fingers working deftly, his head lowered. 'I don't want to end this now,' he said after a moment, and Lucia's breath hitched, her heart lurched.

It was more than he'd ever admitted to before, and yet it was so damn little. 'When, then?' she made herself ask.

'Does it matter?' Angelo glanced up and she saw impatience flicker in his grey-green eyes. Clearly he hadn't expected this conversation to take so long. '*Dio*, Lucia, after last night—you want to go back to your job? Your life?'

She recoiled, stung by the contempt in his tone. 'I think you rate yourself a little too highly,' she managed through stiff lips.

'I'm saying this all wrong.' He shook his head, still impatient. 'Come have breakfast and we'll talk.'

She glanced at the clock. 'I don't really have time—'

'You don't have time? Don't you think this—us— warrants a little more consideration?'

She let out a hollow laugh. 'There's never been an us, Angelo. You made sure about that.'

'It's different now.'

'Because you want it to be?'

'Why are you angry?' He shook his head, angry now himself. 'I'm offering you something I've—'

'Never offered before?' she filled in, her voice hard. 'So I should grab it with both hands and tell you how thankful I am? Sorry I'm not falling in with your plans.'

His expression shuttered, his jaw bunched. 'At least come and eat something,' he said tightly, and brought a tray of fresh fruit and coffee out towards the veranda.

Slowly Lucia followed him outside, wondered why she was so angry. Surely Angelo was doing everything she'd once dreamt about. Incredible sex, making breakfast, wanting to be with her? What was wrong with this picture?

Because she knew instinctively something was.

Outside the day was already hot, the sun beating down, a slight breeze off the sea the only relief. She sank into a chair and mutely accepted the cup of espresso Angelo handed her.

'So tell me what exactly it is you're offering, Angelo,' she said after she'd taken a sip. 'Why should I take a day off work? What are you suggesting?'

'I'm not suggesting you take the day off, although I suppose that would be a start.'

'A start? To what?'

'To—to us!' He looked, quite suddenly, furious—although whether with her or himself she didn't know. She did know, knew with the unshakeable certainty that she'd always possessed when it came to this man, that he still didn't want to want her. Nothing really had changed except, perhaps, the force of Angelo's reluctant need.

'Us,' she repeated. 'What kind of us?'

'Why are you asking all these questions?'

'Because I want to know what you're suggesting, Angelo. You've been barking out orders since I came downstairs but I still don't know what you want. A day in bed? A *relationship*?'

Shamefully her voice trembled on that revealing word, and from the way he quickly averted his gaze she knew it wasn't that. Never that. He still didn't want a relationship, something real, with her.

He didn't say anything for a long moment, just stared out at the sea, his eyes narrowed against the glare of the sun. 'I don't want you working like that any more,' he finally said, and her mouth dropped open before she thought to snap it shut.

'I don't know which part of that sentence to address,' she finally said, her voice thankfully tart. 'It doesn't matter what you want, and as for whatever *like that* means—'

'On your knees, scrubbing—'

'Since I'm no longer working for the Correttis, it

should hardly matter,' she snapped. 'I'm on my knees for you, Angelo.' And ridiculously she felt a blush heat her face at the suggestiveness of her words, the memory of last night.

Angelo leaned forward, his gaze snapping back to hers, his eyes like molten silver. 'Didn't last night mean anything to you, Lucia? Didn't it change anything?'

She swallowed dryly, memories flashing through her mind, making her blush all the more. 'I never got a chance to ask you those questions the last time we spent a night together,' she replied after a moment, 'but I think I could have guessed what the answers would have been.'

Realisation flared in his eyes and he sat back. 'Are you saying last night was—was just a repeat of what happened before?'

'Wasn't it?'

He didn't answer for a long moment, just stared at her, his gaze sweeping searchingly over her. 'Not for me.'

Her fingers tightened on the cup of coffee and she felt the hot liquid slosh over her fingers. Shakily she put it back on the table with a clatter. 'Just what are you saying, Angelo?'

His mouth firmed, his gaze flicking away before returning to rest on her resolutely. 'I told you, I don't want this to end now.'

What a telling phrase, she thought bleakly. Not now, but maybe later. Definitely later. 'When, then?' she asked, striving to keep her voice even.

He shrugged, the movement dismissive. 'I don't know.'

'When you want it to be over?' she surmised flatly.

'*Dio*, Lucia, isn't it enough that I want to be with you? I want to protect you, provide for you. I can give you so much—'

She felt herself go cold. 'Such as?'

'Clothes, jewels, a villa, a car—whatever you want!'
He smiled, relief flashing in his eyes, as if he were glad
they were finally understanding each other. 'You don't
have to work as a maid. You don't have to work at all.
You can live here—'

'And await your pleasure?'

He recoiled, his mouth hardening into a thin line.
'You make it sound…sordid.'

'You're the one doing that, Angelo.' Her voice trembled and she fought against the absurd yearning she still
felt, the temptation to accept even this little. She sat back
in her chair and closed her eyes. She felt near to crying,
and yet too weary to shed any tears.

'I want,' Angelo answered, an edge to his voice now,
'to be with you. You could stay here,' he continued,
sweeping one arm out to encompass the villa. 'You could
have a maid of your own, an entire staff, clothes and jewels. I'll buy you a car, whatever one you like.'

'I don't know how to drive,' she said flatly. 'And I
don't like this villa. I told you that last night. It feels
cold.'

He stared at her incredulously. 'Then I'll hire a driver.
I'll buy a new villa—you can choose it yourself.'

She shook her head. It wasn't just the villa that was
cold; it was the man himself. She didn't know this man
any more. She might have had the most incredible, intimate sex with him last night, but this morning he was
again a stranger.

A stranger who still could only see what he wanted
from her and the most expedient way to get it. Forget
asking her out. Forget even a normal, caring conversation. Even now, when he was trying to be thoughtful,
clearly expecting her to be pleased with these tawdry

suggestions. He had no consideration of her feelings at all, and he didn't even realise it.

Everything in her aching, Lucia rose from the table. 'I need to go to work.'

'I told you, they're not expecting you,' Angelo snapped. He rose from the table, braced his hands on it. His body was taut with emotion, with anger, his mouth a compressed line, his eyes narrowed. 'Lucia, I can see I'm saying all the wrong things. I swear to you, I am not trying to make you angry.'

Which somehow made it worse. He didn't even realise how awful, how *offensive*, his suggestions were. 'I know you're not, Angelo,' she said wearily, and turned away.

He smacked the table with the palm of his hand, rattling the dishes, the crack of his palm echoing through the still air. '*Dio*, don't walk away from me! I'm not done talking to you!'

She stiffened at the autocratic bark of his voice. 'I'm done,' she said flatly. 'And unless you intend to order me not to work as my employer, we have nothing more to say here.'

He stared at her, his eyes flashing with fury, his body tight with suppressed rage, and then on leaden legs Lucia turned and walked back into the house and then out the front door.

Angelo watched Lucia walk away from him in a kind of dazed incredulity. He had not expected this. He still couldn't believe it was happening. She was actually *rejecting* him.

He drove his fingers through his hair, swore under his breath. What was wrong with the woman? He was offering her so much more than she'd ever had before, so much more than she'd ever had with him. He'd spent most of last night awake with her in his arms, trying to think through his own feelings. His own desires. After what they had shared, he knew he wasn't ready to walk away. He didn't think she was either. So he came up with a solution—a solution to give her everything she'd ever wanted—and she refused him?

She was mad.

No, he realised suddenly, the insight causing him to tense, she wasn't. She was angry, because he *hadn't* offered her everything she'd ever wanted. If he had, she surely would have accepted it. So what more did she want?

Swearing again, he strode from the veranda. It took him all of two minutes to ascertain that she'd actually left the villa. Considering the house was miles from so much as a petrol station and she must have known it, the choice to leave on foot was beyond absurd.

Angelo threw open the door of the villa and saw Lucia trudging down the dusty drive. 'Lucia!' he shouted, exasperated with her, with himself, with how this whole morning had unravelled. He'd been looking forward to spending the day in bed, or perhaps again in the shower. He'd been anticipating her incredulous, wondering smile when he'd told her he wasn't walking away.

Instead *she* was walking away…was that what she wanted? Was this actually some kind of *revenge*? God only knew he understood about wanting revenge, yet he could hardly believe it of Lucia.

'Lucia!' he shouted again, and she stilled. Her head came up, her shoulders stiffened and slowly she turned around. 'You cannot walk to Palermo from here,' he called, trying to sound reasonable. 'If you insist on going into work, then let me at least drive you.'

She folded her arms, didn't move. 'Fine,' she called back flatly.

Realising she was simply going to stand there and wait, Angelo swore again under his breath and went back into the house. He pulled on a pair of jeans and leather loafers, grabbed his car keys and headed out. Lucia was waiting by the passenger door of his Porsche, her expression completely unreadable.

Was this the same woman who had cried in his arms last night, both with sorrow and joy, who had told him about their daughter, who had brought him more physical pleasure than he'd had in years…or even ever?

She looked like a stranger. And she acted like a stranger as she slid into the passenger seat and kept her face turned to the window as he started the car.

'It is obvious that I've offended you somehow with my suggestion,' Angelo stated tersely as he headed down the drive. She didn't answer, and he smacked the steering wheel with the palm of his hand. 'At least talk to me, Lucia.'

'I don't think I have anything to say that you'd want to hear.'

That didn't sound good. Angelo blew out a breath. 'I want to hear what you're thinking.'

'Do you really, Angelo? Or will that just make you angrier, because I'm not falling into line with your plans? I'm not falling into your bed.'

'You fell into my bed last night,' he snapped, and then could have cursed himself. *Not* a helpful observation to make at this point.

Lucia kept her face to the window. 'I did,' she said quietly, 'and I don't regret it. But that's all I ever intended last night to be. One night, just as before. I'm not going to be your—your long-term booty call.'

'That is offensive.'

'No kidding.'

His fingers clenched the steering wheel so hard his knuckles whitened. 'You told me that a one-night stand was not something you'd be willing to repeat.'

'I changed my mind.'

'And I changed my mind,' he answered back. 'So you see, we both can change.'

'You think you can change?' She turned to him, eyebrows raised, her tone utterly disbelieving. 'You think, with this suggestion, you *have* changed?'

He forced back the instinctive anger at her incredulous, almost sneering tone. 'You obviously don't think I have,' he said levelly.

She shook her head, folded her arms, the stance clearly one of rejection. 'One night, one week, one month. There's not much difference, Angelo.'

He pressed his lips together and stared straight ahead. All right, he saw her point, but hell, this was new territory for him. He didn't *do* relationships. He didn't have girlfriends or even mistresses. His entire life he'd been focused on work, driven by success and revenge. He had no time for the messy sprawl of romance or, God forbid, *love*. Sex had always been a transaction—

And, he realised, he was proposing such a transaction to Lucia now. He'd dressed it up a bit, yes, but essentially it was a business deal. A bargain.

But he didn't *do* anything else. This was all he had to offer, and damn it, he wanted her to accept it. It wasn't, he thought grimly, such a bad deal.

He glanced at her now, saw she'd turned back to the window. All he could see was the smooth, round curve of her cheek, her plaited hair revealing the vulnerable nape of her neck.

He let out a weary breath. 'Why put a time limit on it, Lucia?' he said, and although she didn't turn from the window he saw her mouth curve in the barest of sad smiles.

'You already did.'

'I did not.' He shook his head, denying the judgement he felt from her. What would make her see sense? 'We didn't use protection last night,' he said after a moment. It hadn't even occurred to him, much to his own shame. 'What if you're pregnant?'

He saw her tense, felt it. 'I don't think that's a possibility.'

'You're on birth control?' Absurd to feel jealous if she was, yet he did. Had she had many other lovers?

'No,' Lucia said after a moment. 'But I—I don't think it's likely.'

'And if it is?'

She turned to him, her expression utterly unreadable. 'You think a pregnancy would force my hand? Make me agree to your…suggestion?'

'It's not such a bad suggestion, Lucia.'

'I think it is.'

'What do you want? Marriage?' He injected the word with the contempt he couldn't help but feel, and he saw hurt flash across her face. *Damn it.*

'And if I did?' she asked quietly.

'I'm not capable of that. I thought—I thought you knew that.'

Her mouth twisted in something like a smile. 'You speak as though it's a chronic condition.'

'I can't help who I am, Lucia.'

'Exactly.'

Frustration bubbled inside him, an unholy ferment of emotion. She was twisting everything he said, taking it completely the wrong way. 'So that's it? You're not even going to give us a chance?'

He heard her draw in a short breath, and knew she was more conflicted, more tempted, than she was trying to act. 'No.'

'*Dio*, Lucia, I think after last night I deserve a little more than that.'

'Did I deserve more than that, before?' she answered. She didn't sound angry though, not the way he felt. She sounded only tired. Resigned, and that made him even more furious. He knew she wanted him. Wanted him as much as he wanted her. Why couldn't she see the sense in what he was offering?

'And so I apologised. I told you I knew I shouldn't have left you like that. God help me, I am trying to make it up to you now. I want to be with you, Lucia. That's what this is about. I thought—I thought you wanted to be with me.' He heard a ragged note enter his voice and stared straight at the road, his jaw so tight he felt as if he might break a tooth. He couldn't believe he was saying these things, much less meaning them.

It felt awful, this helpless confession, like peeling back his own skin. He was raw, vulnerable and completely exposed. And yet still he couldn't help himself. He *had* to say these things. He meant them utterly. He wanted more with Lucia. And yet looking at her averted face he knew his more was still less than what Lucia wanted.

I want to be with you. For a man like Angelo, it was a huge confession. She'd never imagined that he would consider last night the start of something. It hadn't even crossed her mind, because he'd never even hinted at such a thing before. Never remotely wanted it.

And even though it was an amazing admission for him to make, it wasn't enough. It wasn't enough because he didn't even realise how little it was.

Yet Lucia still felt a longing open inside her, that old, endless ache, and she was so unbearably tempted to snatch his paltry offer with both hands. She would have accepted it before. She would have taken whatever crumb he tossed her way, and forced it to sustain her. It was this understanding of her own weakness that made her stiffen her shoulders, harden her resolve.

She really had changed, and she wouldn't let herself accept Angelo's offer of being nothing more than a mistress, even if he hadn't used that word. Even if he didn't understand that was what he was suggesting.

'Lucia,' he said again, his voice still revealingly ragged. 'Say something, please.'

She leaned her head back against the seat and closed her eyes. Willed herself not to say yes...yes, she'd do it, she'd take it, just as long as she could be with him. She would not be that pathetic creature again. Surely she'd had enough rejection for one life.

She'd heard how her mother had begged her father to stay, never mind the drinking, the abuse, the other women. Watched her mother spiral down into despair and bitterness in the following years. Did she really want to be like that?

She had no illusions about how little Angelo was capable of. He'd been pushing people away his whole life. Pushing *her* away. Seven years ago it had been one night; this time it might be a week, a month, perhaps a little longer. And then? He'd push. He'd walk away just as he had before, without a backwards glance. Without even a thought.

'I did want to be with you, Angelo,' she said in a low voice, each word formed with painful effort. 'Once.'

'And not now?'

She swallowed, forced the single word past stiff lips. 'No.'

With her eyes still closed, she didn't see him turn the steering wheel. She just heard the squeal of the tyres and felt her body flung sideways as he pulled the car onto the side of the dusty road. Her eyes flew open and she stared at him in shock, saw his chest rise and fall with ragged breaths as he stared straight ahead.

'Damn it, Lucia,' he said, 'that is *not* true.' He turned to her, his eyes blazing grim determination. 'Look me in the eye and tell me you don't want to be with me. Right here, look me in the eye and swear on your mother's grave—no, on our *daughter's* grave that last night meant nothing to you.'

Lucia stared at him, opened her mouth. No words came out. She couldn't say that, couldn't mean it, and he knew it. 'What do you want from me, Angelo?' she whispered.

'The truth.'

'*Why?*' she burst out. 'Does it stroke your ego to know how much I loved you once? How much I still love you?' She saw shock blaze across his face and his jaw dropped. She laughed, the sound high and wild. 'Yes, I love you. I've always loved you. I loved you when we were children, when I waited for you on my doorstep with a damp cloth for your cuts. I loved you when you told me your dreams of leaving Caltarione, all of Sicily, to make your fortune. I dreamt you'd take me with you, and when you left I still dreamt you'd come back for me. And then you did come back for me—' She broke off, drew in a clogged breath. She was saying so much more than she'd ever intended to reveal, and yet even now she couldn't believe he'd never known. It had been so appallingly obvious to her.

'Lucia—' he said hoarsely, and she flung up one hand.

'*No*. I'll say this now, only now, only once. Loving you doesn't matter. It doesn't make a difference, because I know—I've always known—you don't love me back the same way. You don't love me at all.' He opened his mouth to say—what? Was he actually going to deny something that was so blatantly, brutally true? 'You might think you feel something for me,' she cut him off, 'and perhaps you do. Affection, attraction, something so paltry it hardly matters. I mean no more to you than one of your cars or villas or perhaps one of your corporate takeovers. Something to be acquired, enjoyed and then discarded. That's how you've *always* seen me, Angelo.'

Angelo just stared at her, unspeaking. He still looked dazed.

And he obviously had no answer, for after a few silent seconds he put the car into Drive and swung back onto the motorway, all without a word. Lucia leaned her head back against her seat and closed her eyes. Angelo's silence hurt her far more than she knew it should. Had she actually been expecting him to deny the truth? Hoping for him to insist she was wrong, he really had changed, and he knew now that he loved her?

Fantasies.

Neither of them spoke for the rest of the trip back to Palermo.

Angelo still didn't speak as he pulled in front of the hotel and waited for Lucia to get out. He was still spinning from what she'd said. All of it too incredible, too *much*. He felt too much.

And he'd said too much…more than he'd ever admitted before to anyone *ever*, and she'd thrown it all back in his face. Fury churned through him, along with the shock and the disbelief.

Lucia hesitated as she climbed out of the Porsche, her face still averted, her head bowed. For a second he thought she'd say something—but what? She'd said everything on the side of the road, when she'd told him she loved him and it didn't matter.

Because he didn't love her.

He waited until she'd disappeared into the hotel, and then he pulled away from the kerb with an angry screech of tyres.

His mind a haze, he drove through the crowded streets of Palermo and then along the ocean road towards Messina until he found a deserted stretch of beach. He parked the car on a patch of dry grass along the road and tossed his loafers in the car.

He didn't know how long he walked along the beach, his hands shoved in his pockets, his mind numb. He had meetings to attend, pressure to put on the different Corretti factions. Hell, he had a coup to stage and here he was beachcombing.

Yet still he walked.

I love you. I've always loved you.

How could she love him? Nobody loved him. Nobody had ever told him they loved him before. Not his stony-faced grandparents, not his absent mother and certainly not the father who would have preferred he'd never existed at all.

All you were meant to be was a stain on the sheets.

He'd stopped expecting or even hoping for love or anything close to it long ago. He might have suspected Lucia had had some kind of schoolgirl crush on him at one point, but that's all it had been. It hadn't been real; it hadn't been *love*. It simply wasn't possible.

And he didn't love her. He didn't know how to love, didn't have it in him. He'd accepted that too, understood that about himself. He hadn't loved anyone in his life, hadn't let himself, and so his emotions had atrophied into nothing, an atrophy of the heart. Some might view his lack of love as a weakness or deficiency, but he'd turned it into a strength. If you didn't love anyone it was easier to focus on work, to live for it. Easier to not care when no one loved you back, easier to walk away.

Except now he didn't want to walk away. Lucia was the one walking, and the thought filled him with frustration, fury—and fear. Why couldn't she accept what he'd offered? Why couldn't it be enough for her? It was a hell of a lot more than he'd offered seven years ago, and yet she still wanted more? From him?

Didn't she realise he didn't have any more to give?

Angelo sank onto the sand, his head in his hands. Yes, he realised hollowly, she did, and that was why she'd gone.

He didn't know how long he sat there, unmoving, his mind retreating into numbness once more. Eventually he stirred, saw the sun was high overhead and realised he'd missed at least one, probably two, important meetings.

Resolutely he rose from the sand. He'd spent enough time thinking about Lucia. She didn't want to have an affair? Fine, no problem. There were plenty of other women who did, and in any case he'd gone before without women or sex. Work—revenge—had been his companion, his lover, and it would be again.

He didn't need Lucia.

Seeing her again, he acknowledged, learning about Angelica, all of it had weakened his resolve. Made him want things he knew he couldn't have. That kind of life wasn't for him, could never be for him. It was better this way. It would have to be.

An hour later he was in the corporate offices of the Corretti Hotel, dressed in a designer suit of grey pin-striped silk, about to confirm a meeting with the share-holders of Luca Corretti's fashion company, Corretti Designs. He'd been buying up stock in the company for several months now, quietly, unnoticed by the other shareholders and, it seemed, by even Luca himself. He didn't have enough to stage a takeover like he had with the hotel, but with Luca absent he was going to take the opportunity to put a little pressure on the other share-holders. Hell, maybe they'd even agree to unseat Luca and make him CEO. He already had the hotel after all. It would bring him one step closer to his ultimate revenge.

It was time to think about business—and stop think-ing about Lucia, or love. This was why he'd returned to Sicily, what he'd always wanted. His face now set into familiar harsh lines of determination, Angelo reached for the phone.

CHAPTER EIGHT

SHE WAS DOING the right thing. Lucia repeated that to herself as she walked into the hotel on unsteady legs, everything around her a blur. *She was doing the right thing.* Leaving Angelo, refusing his offer, was the right choice. It had to be, because if one night had nearly felled her seven years ago, what would a week do now? A month? However long Angelo decided he wanted to be with her, all on his terms. *I don't want this to end now.*

Not now, but at some point, yes. He would decide to end it at some point in the not-too-distant future, and when that moment came he would walk away just as before. Just as he always did.

She worked steadily through the morning, grateful to scrub and sweep and spray down counters, and not have to think. Wonder. *Regret.*

She was doing the right thing.

She kept repeating that to herself, a desperate mantra, throughout the next few days. She didn't see or hear from Angelo, and from the sinking disappointment she felt at his absence she knew at least a part of her had been hoping to, even as she knew, bone-deep, that she never would.

Three days after she left Angelo, Maria found her

at break time, sitting alone at a table, lost in her own thoughts.

'Lucia?' The older woman smiled uncertainly, a sheet of paper clutched to her chest.

'*Ciao*, Maria.' Lucia did her best to smile and push away the tangled thoughts about Angelo that turned everything inside her into knots of doubt. 'Did Stefano send you another letter?'

'Not yet, but I want to write him.'

'Again?' Just a few days ago she'd helped Maria write a rather gushing response to Stefano.

Maria nodded, determination glinting in her deep brown eyes. 'Yes… He's not so good a writer, yes? So I keep writing, because I love him.'

The simple, heartfelt statement made Lucia still, those tangled knots inside her loosening just a little. *I keep writing, because I love him.* Maria's love didn't change, no matter Stefano's response—or lack of it. Of course, a mother's love for a son was different from a woman's love for a man, but…

Did she—had she—loved Angelo like that? For years she'd told herself she had, yet she'd never sent him a single letter. Not after he'd left at eighteen, and not seven years later when he'd left her bed. She'd tried, of course, when she'd found out she was pregnant. She'd written draft after labourious draft, yet she hadn't sent a single one. She hadn't got so far as putting any of them in an envelope. She'd never, Lucia saw now with a cringing insight, intended on writing him at all.

Why?

'Lucia?'

'Yes…sorry. Of course I'll help you write him.' She gestured to the seat next to her and Maria sat down, putting the single sheet of paper on the table and smoothing it carefully before handing Lucia a pen. 'What would you like to say?'

Maria smiled shyly. 'Just that I love him. I miss him. I pray for him.' Obediently Lucia wrote this all down, with Maria gazing at her neat handwriting in a kind of incredulous admiration. 'And also that my arthritis, it's better. In case he worries.'

Lucia glanced up, smiling, her eyebrows raised. 'Is it better, Maria?'

The older woman shrugged this aside. 'It's not so bad.'

Lucia wondered if Stefano would think about his mother's arthritis at all. She'd never met the man, and yet she wondered. Doubted. She felt her cynicism coat her heart like a hardened shell, layers and layers built up over time and weary experience. She'd been cynical about Angelo for so long, almost right from the beginning.

She still remembered when he'd left Sicily, how he'd kissed her cheek and turned away, heading off into his far-off future. She'd been seventeen, utterly in love, and she'd told herself if he looked back just once it meant he'd come back for her. He hadn't, and remembering now she knew she hadn't really expected him to. Cynicism coupled with a rather desperate hope—an awful combination. Yet that's how she'd always been with Angelo, wanting something she was quite sure he didn't have to give.

That's how she'd been with him now, when she'd rejected his offer. What if she'd reacted differently? Would Angelo have been able to change? Could they have a chance, if she gave them—him—one?

'I hope he writes you back this time,' Lucia said as she finished the letter, and Maria shrugged, lifted her chin.

'He's a good boy. And even if he doesn't write, he'll always know I love him. That's what matters.'

Lucia felt her throat go tight. 'Yes,' she agreed quietly, 'that's what matters.'

From the shock that had blazed across Angelo's face, she knew he hadn't ever realised she loved him. She'd loved him for years, decades, and yet he'd never known. She'd never told him before, and when she finally had, it had been in anger and exasperation, just another means to push him away.

Yet she *had* to push him away—because if she didn't, he'd surely break her heart.

'It's painfully clear that the Corretti empire is falling apart.' Angelo gazed steadily at each shareholder in turn, watched them fidget and squirm, their uneasy gazes sliding away from his. 'The Correttis simply aren't capable any longer, and the world is noticing.'

More squirming. None of the shareholders at this meeting were related to the Correttis, yet they'd always been loyal. Angelo knew he was taking a risk asking them to switch their loyalty to him, a Corretti of a different kind. He'd called this meeting of shareholders of Corretti Designs in Palermo, knowing that Luca was out of the country. He didn't think it would take too much to nudge the rest of the shareholders into a vote removing Luca as CEO and putting him in his place. They were like dominoes, waiting to fall. And another piece of the Corretti pie would be his. 'The price of Corretti Designs' shares have fallen three per cent in the past week alone,' he continued, knowing that hard facts might sway them more than sly innuendo. 'And it will continue to fall while the Correttis scramble, mired as they are in their own scandal.'

One of the shareholders, a banker from Milan, met his gaze. 'What do you propose?'

'You make me CEO on a trial basis,' Angelo answered swiftly. 'If the share prices improve—'

'The shares have gone down because of the cancelled wedding,' a sharp-looking woman objected. 'It's been all the talk. They'll bounce back in time.'

'Scandal usually boosts share prices of glamour industries,' Angelo replied coolly. 'Yet Corretti Designs' shares have fallen.'

He saw the doubt enter the woman's eyes, felt the mood in the room shift. They might be loyal to Luca Corretti, but all that mattered was the bottom line. 'Six weeks,' he said firmly. 'Give me six weeks and I'll turn this company around.' He held each person's gaze, saw doubts turn into certainties, and triumph surged through him. 'Shall we call a vote?'

'Am I interrupting something?'

Angelo stiffened, then turned his head to see Luca Corretti standing in the doorway of the boardroom, his steely gaze arrowing in on him. He smiled and lounged back in his chair. 'So good of you to join us,' he drawled, and saw a flicker of something almost like admiration in Luca's eyes at his sheer audacity.

'So good of you to invite me,' Luca answered dryly, and came into the room. Angelo felt an answering flare of respect for a man he knew he should hate. Luca Corretti was his cousin, the second son of Benito, his own father's brother. He'd lived in a palace, had grown up with every privilege and luxury. Angelo had hated him on principle for most of his life, yet now he couldn't help but respect the man's steely authority.

He might have been able to buy up the flagship hotel in Matteo's absence, but it appeared taking over Luca's fashion enterprise was going to be a little bit more difficult.

Luca set his briefcase on the table, his gaze moving slowly around the room, pinning every uneasy shareholder in his or her place. 'Now,' he said pleasantly, and Angelo heard the unmistakable undercurrent of authority in his voice, 'where were we?'

Twenty minutes later the meeting had ended and Luca was still in charge. Angelo slid his papers back into his attaché, affected an insouciance he didn't really feel.

Luca glanced at him coolly from across the table. 'Foiled this time, Angelo.'

Angelo gave him a hard smile. 'I don't think we've actually ever been introduced.'

'And yet you seem determined on snatching as much of the Corretti empire as you can.'

'Snatching?' Angelo raised his eyebrows. 'It's business, Luca. It always has been.'

Luca closed his briefcase with a decisive snap. 'Business?' he repeated with a shake of his head. 'I don't think so. Not for you.'

Angelo felt everything in him tense as that familiar rage flashed through him. He hated the other man's mocking tone, that superior sneer. 'Trust me,' he answered evenly, 'it's business.' Without another word he stalked from the boardroom, felt the adrenalin course through him as he took the lift down to the street. Once outside he decided to walk off his anger. He headed towards Pretoria Square, his mind racing along with his heart.

He could certainly do without Luca's fashion house. Buying out the Correttis' flagship hotel had been far more a significant coup and he wasn't going to concern himself with a few dresses. And yet he couldn't keep the resentment from lodging inside him like a stone, heavy and hot, burning through him. Snatching indeed.

How he hated the Correttis, with their smug superiority and their complete indifference to a blood relation, simply because he'd been born on the wrong side of the blanket. Not one of them had ever concerned themselves with him or his welfare. Not one of them had ever cared or considered him at all.

As a boy he'd had the most pathetic, useless fantasies about how they'd notice him. His father would find out about his existence and welcome him into the palazzo. His half-brothers and cousins would become his friends. He had, once upon a time, imagined how they'd become his family, his real family. He'd dreamt of how they'd all love him.

But of course no one ever had.

Except Lucia. Lucia loved you.

He stumbled in his stride and righted himself, tried to push that unhelpful thought away. In the past three days, since he'd left Lucia in front of the hotel, she'd never been far from his thoughts. He'd determined to think of it— her—with cold logic; she said she loved him, so either she was lying or she believed she loved him even though she didn't. Couldn't. There were no other possibilities.

Angelo didn't think she had been lying; she had no reason to lie about such a thing. So she must have somehow convinced herself that she loved him, perhaps as some kind of moral justification for their one-night stand.

And if he disabused her of the ridiculous notion? Convinced her that she couldn't actually love him, that such an idea was mere fantasy? Angelo had at first found himself strangely reluctant to consider such an idea. Yet now as he strode towards Pretoria Square and gazed up at the huge marble fountain—the fountain of shame, it had once been called—he thought again.

Why not? Why not convince Lucia she couldn't love him? Once she let go of such ridiculous, romantic notions she might be more willing to embark on what he wanted: a mutually pleasurable affair. He could still get what he wanted. What she wanted… He just had to convince her that she did.

Lucia was just reaching for another stack of linens when she heard a voice behind her.

'There you are.'

She turned and felt her heart stop right in her chest at the sight of Angelo in the doorway of one of the hotel's supply closets.

'What are you doing here?'

'I need to talk to you.'

'Here? People will talk, Angelo.'

'Let them.'

'Easy for you to say.'

'You never used to care what people thought, Lucia. Remember?' His voice was a rough caress and he stepped into the little room, seeming to take up all the space and air. 'You told me not to care what people thought. What they said to me.'

She focused on counting pillowcases, but in her mind's eye she could see Angelo at ten, eleven years old, bloody and defiant, angry and proud. She remembered trying to tease him out of his hurt, coming up with ridiculous taunts for the ignorant schoolchildren who refused to think of him as anything but the Corretti bastard, the son of a woman they'd said was no better than a whore. More often than not Angelo had just shrugged her off, but once in a while she'd succeeded in making him smile, even laugh. He'd meet her gaze and they'd grin at each other, both of them hurting and yet happy in that moment, united in their understanding of how harsh and unfair the world really was.

'That was a long time ago, Angelo.' Her voice sounded clogged and she cleared her throat, kept her gaze firmly on the sheets and not on the man who seemed intent on breaking her. Again.

'Not so long.' Angelo put one hand on her wrist, stilling her, his touch sure and strong and yet also gentle. 'You don't love me, Lucia.'

She turned to him, surprise temporarily wiping away every other emotion. 'You came here to tell me that?'

'You think you do, but you don't.' He gazed at her steadily, his eyes dark and serious, his tone so very certain.

Lucia shook her head slowly. 'How on earth could you know a thing like that, Angelo?'

'Because.' He frowned, as if he hadn't ever considered the question before. 'Because you can't.'

'I can't,' Lucia repeated. She searched the harsh lines of his face, tried to find some clue as to why he felt the need to tell her this now. 'Does it ease your conscience somehow, to think I didn't love you?'

'It's not about my conscience.'

'What, then?'

The sound of someone pushing a cart came from the corridor, squeaky wheels and a heavy tread. Angelo's breath released in an impatient hiss. 'We can't have this conversation here.'

'I'm working...'

He opened his mouth and she knew he wanted to order her to stop; it was certainly within his rights as her employer. 'When do you get off your shift?' he asked instead, the words coming reluctantly.

'At six.'

'Let me pick you up—'

'And take me back to your villa?' Lucia finished. She felt herself flush and she knew from the answering heat in Angelo's gaze that they were both remembering what had happened the last time they'd done that.

'Then we'll go somewhere else,' Angelo said. 'Out to dinner.'

'A date?' she mocked, even though it hurt. 'Why bother, Angelo? We have nothing more to say to each other.'

'I have something to say to you.'

She stared at the steely glint in his grey-green eyes, and suddenly she remembered her conversation with Maria earlier in the day. *He knows I love him. That's what matters.*

She'd spent so much time and effort pushing Angelo away. What if she stopped? Instead of bearing her love for him like a burden, she'd wear it as a badge.

You'll only get more hurt.

She'd already experienced so much heartache, and yet she'd survived. She was strong; just as Angelo had said. Tragedy had made her stronger.

Yet strong enough for this? To risk her heart one more time, and this more than ever?

She swallowed, made herself nod. 'All right, then.' She turned back to the stacks of sheets. 'You can meet me at the Borgo Vecchio.' She wondered if he'd remember the last time they'd gone to one of Palermo's outdoor markets.

'The Borgo Vecchio? It's no more than a street fair.'

She turned back to him, eyebrows raised. 'Are you too good for a street fair?'

'No, of course not.' Annoyance flashed across his features. 'I just don't see why.'

Obviously he didn't remember. It hadn't been important, at least not important to him. 'I don't belong in fancy restaurants,' she told him. 'And I won't be paraded about Palermo as your whore.'

He recoiled. 'Is that how you see it, Lucia?'

'It's how others see it,' she answered flatly. She saw the surprise in his eyes and knew he hadn't known, had never realised. Never thought for one moment how her pregnancy and his abandonment would have affected her standing in a tiny place like Caltarione.

God help her, what was she doing? How could she risk this—her heart, her life—with a man who had so little consideration or concern for her?

'I didn't realise,' he said quietly. He pressed his lips together, his gaze averted. 'I think there are most likely a lot of things I haven't realised.'

Surprise silenced her. Already he was changing, just a little, but for now she would let it be enough. 'The market?' she prompted, and he nodded.

'I'll meet you at the Borgo Vecchio, a little after six.'

Lucia nodded back, her heart pounding with both dread and anticipation. Yet in the midst of those turbulent emotions she felt a fragile seed sprout to tremulous, trembling life: hope. She hadn't felt it in a long time, perhaps ever. And yet with one quiet word from Angelo she began to believe…and finally hope that things might change between them.

Angelo paced the narrow street of the Borgo Vecchio where he'd agreed to meet Lucia. Stalls heaped with lemons and oranges as well as cheap clothing and electronics jostled for space with the many pedestrians thronging the side street. The smell of fried fruit wafted on the hot air, competing with the stink of unwashed humanity and the diesel fumes from the cars and mopeds speeding by.

Why the hell had he agreed to meet Lucia here? He could have had a reservation at one of the city's best restaurants, champagne chilling in a bucket, caviar and pâté and whatever else they desired immediately on hand. Seated amidst such luxury would have been a much better setting for a seduction.

Yet was that what he intended on doing? Seducing Lucia? No. He was just convincing her of the truth. Making her see the benefits of a loveless affair.

Still he felt uneasy. Unsure. And he didn't like it. He'd lived his life on clear certainties, hard truths, yet Lucia made him doubt. Wonder. *Want.*

'Hello, Angelo.'

He turned and saw her standing before him, her dark hair pulled back in a neat plait, her eyes clear and somehow sad. She'd exchanged her grey maid's uniform for a cheap cotton sundress in pale pink, and Angelo found his gaze helplessly drawn to the smooth olive skin of her shoulders, the swell of her breasts underneath the snug cotton. He yanked his gaze upwards.

'Thank you for meeting me.'

She nodded, hitched her canvas bag higher up on her shoulder. 'Shall we eat?'

'Eat?' He couldn't keep from sounding rather revolted. 'Here?'

She laughed softly. 'You used to like the pizza here.'

And then a memory flashed through his mind, slotted into place. They'd once taken the bus into Palermo, wandered through this market. They must have been fourteen or so; all Angelo had remembered about that day was the burning anger he'd felt at seeing his half-brothers, Alessandro and Santo, out with their father. A happy family, father and sons, strolling through the narrow streets of Caltarione. They hadn't looked his way once.

Lucia, he remembered now, had suggested the trip into the city, probably as a way to distract him from the Correttis. They'd eaten pizza and gelato, and she'd made silly jokes all the while, betting him she could eat more pizza than he could, and he, of course, had proved her wrong. But she'd succeeded in making him laugh, which had surely been her object all along.

Dio, he missed that. Laughing with someone, being stupid and silly and *real*. Lucia, he acknowledged with sudden, flashing insight, was the only person in the entire world with whom he'd ever been remotely real.

'I remember,' he said now, quietly, and he saw her mouth curve in the slightest of smiles.

She turned away, and the end of her plait brushed his shoulder. 'So, pizza?' she asked, and he fell in step beside her.

'Pizza, it is.'

They settled for squares of *sfincione*, the doughy Sicilian pizza scattered with bread crumbs, cheese and anchovies. Angelo eyed his sauce-covered square somewhat dubiously. 'We could be eating fresh flounder at one of the city's best restaurants,' he told her, not even half joking, and she shook her head.

'I wouldn't even know what fork to use.'

It wasn't the first time she'd made a remark alluding to the difference in their stations now, and he wondered at it. 'I'm sure you'd figure it out pretty quickly. And in any case, when you're eating in a restaurant, use whatever the hell fork you want.'

She gave a little laugh. 'That would be your attitude.'
'It would.'

She eyed him over her pizza, her eyes wide and so very blue. 'Why do you think I don't love you, Angelo?' she asked quietly.

Angelo felt something in him shift, lurch. He had the strangest, strongest impulse to deny it, to convince her of the opposite, that she did love him. He swallowed a bite of pizza and shifted his gaze a few inches to the right of her face. 'Because you don't.'

'That's not an answer and you know it.' He just shrugged. He hadn't thought through this very well, he realised. He had no arguments to make beyond what to him was the appallingly obvious: she *couldn't* love him. All on its own it wasn't very compelling. 'How can you say what I feel, or if I really feel it?' she pressed.

'How do you know you love me?' Angelo challenged. 'How can you be sure?'

He shifted his gaze back to her face, saw how still she'd gone, trapped by truth. She *wasn't* sure. Damn it if he didn't feel disappointed. She swallowed, licked her lips, causing a shaft of pure desire to streak through him. Even now, amidst a painfully awkward conversation about emotions, he wanted her. Forget talking. Forget love or lack of it. He'd just haul her into his arms and kiss her until they were both senseless.

'I know I love you,' she said slowly, quietly, 'because whenever I'm with you I feel complete and whole. And when you're gone, I don't.'

Angelo felt his jaw go slack, everything inside him seeming to shut down. He had no words; he had no thoughts. 'You've been living without me for fifteen years,' he finally managed, his voice hoarse, and she smiled sadly.

'I know.' He shook his head, his instinct, his *need*, to deny. 'Tell me this, Angelo,' she cut off whatever unformed reply he'd been going to make. 'Why don't you want me to love you? I'm not asking for anything back. I'm not making demands or a scene. I'm not doing or expecting anything.' She smiled, the corners of her soft mouth curving up tremulously. 'So what scares you about my loving you? About love?'

Everything. He didn't answer, just shook his head. Again. 'You can't love me, Lucia,' he said. He sounded like a broken record, but hell, he didn't *have* anything else.

'You didn't answer my question.'

'That *is* the answer.'

'All right,' she said evenly, 'I'll ask a different question. Why do you think I can't love you? And I want something more than "because."' He heard a slight quaver in her voice, and knew, despite her quiet, utter sincerity, this was hard for her. Maybe as hard for her as it was for him. And he knew then if she could be honest enough to admit that she loved him, then he could be honest enough to admit why he didn't think she could.

'Because,' he said, his gaze averted, each word drawn slowly, painfully, from him. 'No one's ever loved me.' He set his jaw, wished the words right back. Could he sound more pathetic, whining about how nobody liked him?

Lucia didn't answer, and he forced himself to meet her gaze, to see the pity that was surely reflected there. He didn't see pity, only sorrow and a surprising determination. 'Then,' she answered, 'I'm lucky to be the first.'

He blinked back the sudden sting of tears. God help him, he was practically *crying*. 'No,' he said, and that was all he could manage. He forced back all that awful emotion and met her gaze once more. 'What is this really, Lucia? When I first saw you in the hotel—when I brought you up to my office—you didn't tell me you loved me then. You wouldn't even admit to being angry at me. You acted like you didn't care about me at all.'

And he'd believed her then. Even now, with everything she'd said, he still believed.

'Loving you,' Lucia said, 'isn't the same as wanting to love you.'

'Ah.' Well, maybe that made sense. Of course she wouldn't *want* to love him.

She sighed and shook her head. 'Angelo, I didn't want to love you because I knew—I know—you don't love me back. Who wants that?'

He shrugged, hating this conversation. 'Nobody, I suppose.'

'Exactly.' She hesitated, and he felt the heaviness of the words she wasn't saying. He just didn't know what they were. 'I said, I *didn't* want to love you,' she said quietly. 'But then, in just the past few days, I started thinking…' She trailed off, biting her lip, and Angelo suddenly, desperately, wanted to know what she'd started thinking about. He *needed* to know.

'You started thinking what?' he asked brusquely.

Her teeth sank in deeper to her lip and he saw cloud-coloured shadows in her eyes, hiding the true emotion underneath. 'I started thinking that maybe I never gave you a chance,' she whispered.

'A chance? A chance for what?'

'To love me.'

The words seemed to hang in the air between them, a hope, a challenge. *A chance to love her.*

What the hell was he supposed to do with that?

'Lucia…'

'I'm not asking you to love me,' she said quickly.

'Not just like that. But…but if you do actually want to be with me, then I won't take some affair, some kind of sordid *arrangement*. If you want to be with me, then you *be* with me. You get to know me again, you ask me out on a date.'

'I did ask you on a date,' he objected, nettled. 'I asked you out to dinner at a proper restaurant.'

'In order to convince me that I don't love you! What was behind that, Angelo? Did you think if I decided I didn't love you, I'd think desire was enough and I'd hop into bed with you? Is that how your twisted mind works?' She spoke with an edge but also with humour, and he actually blushed.

Yes, it appeared that was how his twisted mind worked.

'Love complicates things,' he said defensively. 'It's messy.' And scary. And awful. And loving people usually meant they didn't love you back. They didn't love you at all.

'You think I don't know that?' she answered, still with the edge and the humour. 'My life would have been a whole lot simpler, a lot cleaner, if I'd never loved you.'

He bristled instinctively. 'So don't.'

'I've tried.' She met his gaze squarely, her eyes blazing truth. 'But I can't stop, because I love you too much.'

Her words made him breathless, as if he'd been punched in the gut. He was quite literally winded. 'So why are you telling me this now?' he asked after a moment, when he trusted his voice. 'When you've been denying it all along?'

'Because I decided you should know. I *want* you to know. I'm tired of pretending I've never cared about you, when I do. So very much.' She drew a deep breath and he heard how it shuddered through her. She'd laid every-

thing out there for him, and God help him but he had no
idea what to do with it. What to say. What he wanted.

Her.

'So now it's your turn,' she said, and gazed at him
with a fragile pride, a tremulous determination. 'You
have to decide what you want, Angelo. If you just want
sex, find someone else. If you want a fling or an affair,
don't look at me.' She let out another breath, threw her
shoulders back. Angelo felt a surge of admiration for this
woman who was so strong, so proud, so brave. She'd endured so much already, and yet she remained unbowed.
'But if you want something more, something real…if
you want to give me—us—a chance, then…' She smiled,
barely. 'You know where to find me.'

CHAPTER NINE

IT WAS AMAZING how liberating telling the truth could be. After her painful admission to Angelo last night, Lucia had expected to feel raw, exposed. Uncomfortable, at least, from revealing so much. She hadn't denied or dissembled, hadn't thrown the truth in his face as a defensive ploy. No, she'd given it to him. Presented it to him like a gift, and it was now his to do with as he wished.

The realisation made her feel buoyant. She had nothing more to hide, and it gave her a giddy sense of both relief and joy. Of course she wondered just what he intended to do with her gift, but she refused to let herself become mired in fear or doubt. For the first time her love for Angelo didn't feel like a weakness, a burden to bear. It felt like a strength.

Several chambermaids were huddled in the staff locker room when she arrived at the hotel for work the next morning. They broke apart as soon as they saw her, and Lucia felt a ripple of unease at their suddenly hushed whispers, their averted gazes. Emilia was the only one to look at her directly, and the expression on her face was one of savage jealousy, eyes narrowed and glittering, lips thin and pursed.

'*Ciao,*' Lucia said with an uncertain smile. '*Come va?*'

'Look.' Maria took her by the elbow and brought her

over to a table on the side of the room; a huge bouquet of flowers rested on it. 'For you.'

'Me?' Lucia stared at the gorgeous bouquet—lilies and roses, orchids and carnations. It was the most extravagant, over-the-top bouquet she'd ever seen, and just the sight of it made a silly grin spread over her face. She'd never received so much as a wilted daisy before.

Emilia folded her arms, her eyes sparking maliciously. 'Payment for services rendered, maybe?'

Maria hissed under her breath. '*Stai zitto*, you foolish girl,' she snapped.

For once Emilia's words rolled right off her. Lucia reached for the crisp white card tucked among the blooms and read the message scrawled on it in a bold hand.

> *I want that chance. Have dinner with me tonight at eight?*

Her smile widened even as her heart started beating hard. Chances were wonderful, dangerous things. This could be a chance for Angelo to love her—or break her heart all over again. Shatter it, even, into a million tiny pieces, impossible to put together again, because she'd never given him this kind of chance before. She'd never actually *tried*.

During her midmorning break Lucia took the service lift to the floor of corporate offices. She felt a blush spread across her face as Angelo's personal assistant glanced up at her in cool assessment.

'Is Mr Corretti available?' she asked, to which the secretary merely pursed her lips. 'He might be expecting me,' she added quietly.

'He's in a meeting.'

'Then will you please leave him a message?' Lucia felt the tingly warmth that Angelo's short note had given her spread throughout her body. 'Tell him Lucia said yes.'

The assistant arched her eyebrows, curiosity clearing getting the better of her. 'That's all?'

'That's all.'

She could barely concentrate on her work for the rest of the day; her mind moved dizzily from anticipation to worry to hope, and then back again. She had nothing to wear. What if Angelo took her somewhere fancy? What would they talk about? A *date* with Angelo. An actual date—something they'd never gone on before. What if it went all wrong?

By the time she arrived back at her apartment that evening, she was both exhausted and hyped up with adrenalin. She showered and stood in front of her closet with its paltry few dresses, wishing she had something pretty and feminine to wear. She almost wished she hadn't left the gorgeous clothes Angelo had bought her back in his villa.

Sighing, she reached for a sundress in a pretty, pale blue. It was simple and cheap, and it was all she had. It would have to do. This wasn't about impressing Angelo, she reminded herself as she slipped it on. It wasn't about pretending to be something or someone she wasn't. She wanted him to know and accept who she really was, cheap clothes and all. That was the only kind of chance she was interested in.

She'd just finished her makeup—no more than lipgloss and a little mascara—when she heard a knock on the door. Taking a deep breath, she hurried to open it, and then found she had no words when she caught sight of Angelo standing there, dressed in a white dress shirt open at the throat and a pair of charcoal grey trousers.

He looked effortlessly elegant and deliberately casual, his eyes blazing grey-green in his tanned face.

He smiled as he saw her, and reached for her hand, giving her a little twirl so her dress flared out around her legs. 'You look lovely.'

'It's not much—'

'Just say thank you.'

She laughed softly. 'Thank you.' They stared at each other for a moment, and Lucia tucked her hair—she'd worn it loose—behind her ears. 'I'm nervous,' she confessed, and Angelo dipped his head.

'So am I.'

She gazed at him uncertainly. 'You don't seem nervous.'

'You might be surprised at this,' he answered, a smile in his eyes, 'but I'm rather adept at hiding my emotions.' She laughed again, felt the fizzing tension inside her begin to ease. Angelo tugged on her hand. 'Let's go.'

He led her downstairs to his Porsche parked by the kerb. She slid into the luxurious leather interior, felt that anticipation rise again. 'Where are we going?'

'A little place inland.' He glanced at her with a smile. 'Nothing too fancy.'

She smiled back, reassured yet still nervous. Everything about this felt strange, new and exciting, yes, but *scary*. So scary.

They didn't talk much on the way to the restaurant, the silence between them expectant yet thankfully not too strained. All around them the sky was settling into twilight, and the last blush of sunset lighted the rugged horizon as Angelo pulled into the dirt lot of a small and unassuming building in a tiny hillside village about twenty kilometres from Palermo.

He'd been telling the truth when he said the place was

nothing fancy, just wooden tables and chairs and plain, whitewashed walls, but a single glance at the menu told Lucia that this was still a high-class restaurant, with high-class prices.

'Not too many forks,' Angelo murmured as they were seated to a private table in the back, and she smiled.

'I can just about manage these.'

'I have no doubt about that.'

A waiter appeared and Angelo ordered a bottle of wine while Lucia fidgeted with her napkin, her glass of water. Few forks there might have been, but she still felt outclassed.

'So,' she said when the waiter left, 'fill me in on the past fifteen years.'

Angelo smiled faintly. 'It could be summed up in a few sentences. I worked. I worked some more. I made money.'

'Give me the long version, then. What did you do after you first left Sicily?'

He shrugged, his long, lean fingers toying with his own cutlery, clearly on edge albeit for a different reason. 'I went to Rome. I didn't have any better ideas, to be honest.'

She imagined him in that huge city—a city she'd never seen—with nothing but a rucksack of clothes and his own burning ambition. 'Did you know anybody there?'

He shook his head. 'I got a job running messages for a finance firm. I learned the city and English, saved up for a moped, and then after about a year I started my own business offering the same service, only faster and cheaper.'

'That was quick.' He would have only been nineteen.

'I spent the next couple of years building that business, and I sold it when I was twenty-three. I wanted to move into real estate, and so with the proceeds from that sale I bought a derelict building in an up-and-coming neighbourhood and turned it into a hotel.' He stopped then, and glanced away.

'And then?' Lucia asked after a moment.

Angelo shrugged. 'More of the same. A bigger building, a shopping centre, and so on. Five years ago I moved to New York and started doing the same thing there.'

'And now you're doing it in Sicily.'

He hesitated for a second's pause and then nodded. 'Yes.'

The waiter came with the wine, and Lucia watched as Angelo swirled it in his glass and tasted it. He nodded once, and the waiter began to pour. When had he learned about such luxuries? she wondered. When had he become accustomed to three-thousand-euro suits, fast cars and fancy restaurants? It was all so removed from her own small world, her shabby apartment and her working-class job. How on earth could a relationship between them ever work?

'Taste,' Angelo said, and she picked up her glass. The wine was rich and velvety-smooth, warming her insides.

'Delicious,' she said, although in all honesty she couldn't really tell one wine from another.

'So tell me what you've been doing these past fifteen years, Lucia, besides working.'

She smiled wryly. 'Not much.'

'You must have other pursuits. Hobbies.'

'I like to read.'

'What kind of books?'

'Anything, really. I like…' She felt herself blushing, which was ridiculous, but there it was. 'I like travel books. Memoirs about people going places, seeing things.'

'And would you like to travel yourself, one day?'

'One day, perhaps.' She hadn't yet had the chance.

'Those postcards,' Angelo said slowly, his considering gaze sweeping over her. 'You used to collect postcards from places all over the world.'

'Just the ones nobody wanted any more,' she said quickly, and he chuckled.

'I wasn't accusing you of stealing, Lucia. I'd just forgotten, that's all. You had a scrapbook.'

'Yes.'

'You wanted to go to Paris,' he spoke slowly, as if the memories were surfacing in his mind, popping like bubbles. 'You had a postcard of the Eiffel Tower, didn't you?'

'Yes.'

'We looked at them together.'

'I bored you with them, more like.'

He shook his head. 'No.'

'You don't need to rewrite the past, Angelo,' she said quietly. 'I know well enough how it was.'

He leaned forward, his eyes glittering. 'Then tell me how you think it was, Lucia.'

She glanced down, felt her face warm. '*Mi cucciola*, remember? I was like an annoying little puppy to you, always frisking at your heels. Sometimes you'd pat me on the head and sometimes you'd kick me away.'

He sat back, silent, and she risked a glance upwards. 'I suppose that's true.'

It was absurd to feel hurt by his admission, but she did. She'd always known he hadn't really cared about her, had tolerated her and sometimes enjoyed her company, but that was all. She'd known that absolutely, and yet…it hurt for him to admit it now.

'That was my problem though,' he added quietly, 'not yours.'

'What do you mean?'

He shrugged one powerful shoulder. 'I didn't appreciate you. I didn't realise what I'd had with you until I'd left.'

She swallowed past the ache in her throat. 'You're still rewriting history, Angelo. You can't expect me to believe you even thought of me once while you were buying and selling your businesses.'

He didn't answer, and that ache in her throat spread, strengthened. She swallowed again, trying to ease its pervasive pain. This really shouldn't have hurt. It was no more than she'd always known, even said to him, yet that had been when she'd been trying to convince herself she didn't care. Now that she'd admitted she did, it hurt more.

'You're right,' he finally said. 'I didn't think of you. But that was a choice, and it took more energy and determination than I ever realised to do it.'

'What do you mean?'

'I missed you,' Angelo said simply. 'I may not have realised it at the time, but I missed you, Lucia. I've always missed you.'

And just like that the ache dissolved into a tentative, hopeful warmth. 'I've missed you too,' she said quietly.

'So tell me what else you've been doing these past years,' Angelo said after a moment. He had to clear his throat, and Lucia took a sip of wine. Admitting you missed someone might not seem like much, but she knew to Angelo it was a big deal. He didn't do emotion, and certainly not vulnerability.

'Not much else, really.'

'You were helping that other maid. Maria.'

'Yes—'

'How?'

She shrugged. 'She has trouble with reading and writing, and so I help her with her letters. I know I didn't get much schooling—'

'No less than me.'

She nodded, accepting. They'd both quit school at sixteen; they'd both needed to work. 'I enjoy it, and it helps her.'

'Have you helped others?'

Another shrug. 'A few. A lot of women in my position can barely read or write. I'm fortunate that I can.'

'That's one way of looking at it.'

She frowned. 'What do you mean?'

'Haven't you ever railed against fate, Lucia? Destiny or God, whatever power that left us both poor and struggling, grateful simply for a job that put food on the table?'

She shook her head. 'What would be the point?'

'Perhaps there's no point in railing,' Angelo answered, 'but in wanting. In doing and having—and *being* more.'

She shook her head again. Here was yet another difference between them. Angelo had always been ambitious, determined to rise above their childhood of the struggling working class in a small Sicilian village; she had never even considered such a thing.

Liar. She'd dreamt of Angelo taking her with him when he'd left, or returning for her. Yet she'd always known they were just that: dreams. Nothing more, nothing real. She hadn't really believed in them.

And even now when they were both trying to make those dreams a reality, she wondered if it were possible. Angelo would never fit into her world, and how could she possibly enter his?

He leaned forward. 'What are you thinking about?'

'Just how different we are.'

'That's not a bad thing.'

'No...' she said slowly, because she couldn't classify it that way, good or bad. Difficult, perhaps. Impossible, maybe.

Angelo reached across the table and laced his fingers with hers. 'Deep down, Lucia, we're not as different as you think.'

She met his gaze, felt his fingers squeeze hers. 'Maybe not,' she answered, but she knew she sounded doubtful.

'Just the fact that you kept that scrapbook of postcards tells me you've wanted something more.'

'That doesn't mean I'd shake my fist at the world if I don't get it.'

'I'm not talking about shaking your first.' He glanced down as he slid his fingers along hers, examining each one in turn, and just that simple touch made her heart beat faster and that lovely, languorous warmth spread throughout her whole body. 'I'm talking about doing something about it.'

'You're the only one of us who did something about it, Angelo. You got out, made more of yourself. I never did.'

He glanced up at her, his fingers still twined with hers. 'Do you regret that?'

'I don't see the point of that either.' She swallowed. 'I had obligations here.'

'You mean your mother?'

'Yes—'

'And then,' Angelo said softly, 'our daughter.' She felt herself stiffen, and Angelo's fingers closed gently around hers. 'What had you planned? To raise her in Caltarione?'

She nodded. 'I didn't have anywhere else to go.'

'You could have moved to Palermo. Even that would

have been a bit of a fresh start.' He didn't sound accusing or judgemental, just curious. Wanting to understand her.

'Yes, and I did think of it. But it felt like running away. And I didn't want—' She hesitated, not wanting to admit how bad it had been for her then.

'You didn't want?' Angelo prompted, his fingers still linked with hers.

'I didn't want people to think I'd been beaten. Or that I was ashamed.'

His fingers tightened over hers briefly. 'Is that how people acted? Like you should have been ashamed?'

'An unwed mother in a tiny village? Of course they did.' She'd meant to sound light and wry, but she knew she hadn't managed it. Angelo's face darkened, a frown compressing his mouth.

'And not just an unwed mother. Another Corretti bastard.'

She clenched her fingers into a protective fist. 'How did you know?'

'I guessed. It took me long enough. But I've noticed a few looks…. People know, don't they? Even at the hotel.'

'Only some. But gossip spreads.'

'How did they? How did anyone know I was the father?'

'Oh, Angelo.' She shook her head, smiling even though a lump had lodged in her throat. 'Carlo Corretti's funeral was at the church in Caltarione. You walked all the way from the church down the main street with every old woman—and young too—peeping from behind her curtains. Everyone knew about the funeral, of course. And everyone knew you were there.'

'And everyone,' he finished, 'saw me knock on your door.'

'And come in,' she added with a sad smile, 'and not

leave until morning. I'm amazed both our ears weren't singed by all the gossip.'

Angelo didn't speak for a long moment. He glanced down at their entwined hands, her fingers still pulled protectively into a fist. A tiny movement, pointless, yet some part of her still reacted in self-defence. Carefully he straightened each clenched finger, then laid his palm flat against hers, a warm, comforting weight. 'I should have thought of that,' he said quietly, his gaze still on their pressed palms. 'Back then. I should have considered how it might look for you. Even if you hadn't fallen pregnant, the gossip would have flown.'

'It always does.'

'I should have—'

'What could you have done, Angelo? Your life was in Rome. No matter what might develop between us now, it was still a one-night stand back then.'

He looked up at her, his eyes dark and shadowed. 'Only because I couldn't imagine anything else.'

'What do you mean?'

'This is new territory for me, Lucia.' The smile he gave her was crooked, self-deprecating. 'A relationship of any kind—'

'You must have had relationships before.'

'No.'

'No? None at all?' She frowned, finding that hard to believe. Angelo was thirty-three years old, a man of experience, wealth and power. Of course he'd had relationships.

'I've had…transactions,' Angelo said carefully. 'Of the kind I first suggested to you.' A faint flush touched his cheekbones, and Lucia almost laughed even as his admission made a fresh sorrow sweep through her.

'That sounds like a rather empty way to live.'

'It was. Is. I think…' He paused, his gaze on their hands once more. He slid his fingers through hers, entwining their hands again. 'I think I've always felt empty.'

'Oh, Angelo.' She swallowed, sniffed. He glanced up wryly.

'I didn't mean to make you sad.'

'You haven't, not really.'

'And what about you?' He leaned back, sliding his hand from hers. Self-protection, Lucia knew. He was just starting to realise how much he'd revealed. 'You must have had a few relationships over the years.'

She let out a little laugh of disbelief. 'Oh, Angelo, do you really believe that?'

He frowned. 'Why not?'

'Because of everything I've already said. I've spent my entire life in Caltarione, working as a maid. Every single person there knows my history, my shame, even if I never saw it like that. What self-respecting Sicilian man would want me?'

'I want you,' he said, his voice rough, and she smiled even as a thrill shot through her at the blatant emotion and need visible in his eyes.

'That's certainly enough for me.'

'Still…are you really saying there's been no one? I've been your only lover?' His voice had dropped to a whisper and now Lucia knew she was the one blushing.

'It sounds a bit pathetic, I know.'

'No, not pathetic.' He shook his head. 'It just makes me a little…afraid.'

'Afraid?' She hadn't been expecting that. 'Why?'

'Because most people don't get this kind of second chance, Lucia.' His expression had turned serious, even grave. 'I don't want to wreck it. I don't want to hurt you like I did before.'

She opened her mouth to say—what? What could she say? She had no assurances or promises to make, for she had no idea if he would hurt her or not. No idea if any of this could really work.

Angelo watched the emotions chase across Lucia's face, reveal themselves in her eyes. She was afraid, he knew. Afraid of what? How different they were? Afraid that this—whatever this between them was—wouldn't work? Afraid that he would hurt her, just as he'd said. Certainty lodged inside him, as heavy as a stone. Of course she was afraid of that. So was he.

Her heartfelt admission last night had rocked him to the core, because he'd finally believed her. She *did* love him. It seemed incredible, impossible, and yet he'd believed, and that belief gave life to something far more precious: hope. He wanted a chance to love her back. A chance to show her he was worthy of her love.

Yet already he felt doubt begin its insidious attack on that first, fragile breath of hope. He'd never loved anyone before, didn't know what it felt or looked like, and God help him, he didn't know if he was capable of it. Nothing in his life had prepared him for any of this, not for honesty or vulnerability and certainly not for love. Not even, he realised with a pang, for a conversation like the one they were having right now.

Maybe they needed a break from all this wretched vulnerability. Smiling, he reached for his menu. 'We should order.' Maybe if they kept the conversation light, rather than raking through the cold ashes of the past, the fear they both felt would lessen if not leave them entirely.

Lucia nodded her agreement, and after they'd ordered

their food they spent the next couple of hours chatting about inconsequential things, tasting each other's food and simply enjoying each other's company. Angelo felt himself relax, and more importantly, he felt Lucia relax.

It was late by the time they drove back to Caltarione, and in the darkness of the car Lucia lapsed back into silence once more, staring out the window so Angelo couldn't tell what she was thinking.

'A penny for your thoughts,' he said lightly, although he wasn't sure he wanted to know. As they'd left the restaurant, Lucia's expression had turned pensive, even drawn. Was she regretting this, *him*? Now she just shook her head, and he left it at that.

He climbed the rickety stairs with her to her second-floor apartment, hating the shabby smallness of it all. He wanted to take her to his villa, to give her all the things she'd never even dreamt for herself. Clothes and jewels, yes, but something more. Safety, comfort, the kind of life neither of them had had as children. The kind of life he wanted for her, even if she refused to want it for herself. Giving her those things would be a way to show her he cared, yet he knew she didn't want them, would refuse his offers. She wanted something else—something he didn't know if he had in him to give.

She turned to him in front of the door. 'Do you want to—'

'Come in?' he finished. She looked delectable in her pale blue sundress, the colour a shade lighter than the startling sapphire of her eyes. Her teeth caught her lower lip and she gazed up at him, eyes wide before her lashes swept downwards. 'More than you could possibly know,' he told her gruffly, desire coursing through him in lightning streaks. 'But I won't.'

He was gratified to see disappointment turn down the corners of her mouth. 'Why not?'

Gently he tucked a tendril of hair behind her ear. 'Because I want to do this right, Lucia. I don't want to rush things.' It would be easy, he knew, to let it be about sex. Let their attraction for each other wipe out the need for talking or even thinking. Hell, that would be *much* easier. But he knew she wanted more, and, amazingly, so did he. If he could manage it.

She swallowed and nodded and he leaned forward to brush his lips against hers, allowing himself this much. Yet of course he couldn't stop there. He never had been able to before. One taste of Lucia and he was a drowning man.

Her lips parted beneath his and he deepened the kiss, his hands coming around her shoulders as he pressed against her, losing himself in her warmth and softness so everything else fell away. He slid one knee between her legs, his mouth moving more firmly over hers as he pressed against her.

Behind her the wooden railing gave an almighty crack and, alarmed, Angelo pulled her forward into the shelter of his own body. '*Dio*, this place is falling down around your ears.'

Wrong thing to say. Perhaps even to think. She shook her head and stepped out of his embrace. 'It's my home, Angelo.'

He let out an irritated breath. 'I wasn't trying to insult you.'

'I know that.'

They stared at each other in the darkness, the only sound the tinny music from the bar downstairs, the hitch of their own breathing.

'Come with me,' he said suddenly, 'to the Corretti Cup next week.'

'The Corretti Cup?' she repeated blankly. 'You mean, the horse race?'

He nodded. Gio Corretti, his cousin, ran the island's premier racing track. The Corretti Cup was an important annual event, attended by the rich, the famous, the beautiful, as well as the entire Corretti clan. He'd never gone before, but he certainly intended on showing up this year, and letting the Corretti family tree know they now had to contend with his unfortunate offshoot. He wanted Lucia by his side.

She bit her lip, uncertainty swamping her wide-eyed gaze. 'I don't know, Angelo—'

'You can't hide forever, Lucia.'

'I'm not hiding—'

'Avoiding, then. My world is different from yours now, I know that. But I want you in it. Won't you please come with me?'

She swallowed, and he knew she felt conflicted. Afraid, even, of this too. 'I don't have anything to wear,' she finally said, and he almost laughed with relief.

'That's simple. I'll take you shopping, buy you a dress.'

'I don't—'

'Lucia, I want to buy you something. It would please me. Won't you let me do that?' He didn't know what her difficulty in accepting gifts from him was, but he suspected it stemmed from the inequality she felt in their positions. He had more money than she did, but nothing else had changed. He was, and would always be, the Corretti bastard looking in, wanting more.

Didn't she realise that? He really wasn't any different from the boy she'd fallen in love with…even if he wanted to be. Even if he was determined to show the Correttis and everyone else on this godforsaken island just how damned different he was.

Slowly she nodded. 'All right.'

'We'll go tomorrow, after work.'

'Actually, I have the day off tomorrow.'

'You do?'

She laughed softly. 'It does happen.'

'Then we can spend the day together.'

'Don't you have meetings? Deals to make?'

He had several important meetings, but with only a second's pause he brushed them all aside at the prospect of spending a whole day in Lucia's company. 'I can rearrange my schedule. I'll pick you up at ten.'

She nodded, still hesitant, still shy. 'OK.'

He drew her back towards him, pressed his lips to her forehead. 'It will be OK,' he said, as much to himself as to her.

She didn't pretend to misunderstand. 'You don't know that.'

'We'll take it slowly.'

'I don't think it's the pace that matters.'

He didn't either. He tipped her chin up with his finger so he could meet her clouded gaze. 'What are you afraid of?'

She pressed her lips together, didn't answer, but then she didn't have to. He knew what she was afraid of; he was afraid of it as well.

Was he capable of loving her? Was he capable of love at all?

He didn't know the answer, and he knew Lucia didn't know it either. With one last, soft kiss, he let her go and headed back down the stairs.

CHAPTER TEN

'How about this one?'

Lucia glanced at the skintight leopard print mini-dress Angelo had pulled off the rack and shook her head, laughter bubbling up inside her. 'It's not my colour.'

'Zebra print, maybe?' He took out another dress and this time she laughed aloud.

'I doubt there's been a zebra print dress seen at the Corretti Cup ever.'

'Always time for a first.'

She shook her head, still smiling, and moved down the rack at one of the city's most exclusive boutiques, leopard print dresses and all. They'd visited several boutiques this morning, and her nervousness about being in these exclusive shops with their snooty sales clerks and elegant upholstery had dissolved in the glow of Angelo's smile, the ease of his good humour. She'd forgotten how much fun he could be. It had taken a lot of effort when they were children to make him smile and relax, but when he did…

There was no one with whom she'd rather be.

'All right, since you aren't going to go for the animal prints, how about this?' Angelo had moved to another rack of dresses, these one in various jewel tones.

He pulled out a slim sheath dress of sapphire silk, the fabric possessing an icy glow. Lucia drew in a breath.

'It's lovely,' she said hesitantly, because she couldn't actually imagine wearing it. She couldn't imagine wearing any of these dresses, leopard print included. She felt like a little girl playing dress up, and at any moment someone was going to come in and bark at her to stop pretending. Stop trying to be someone else.

'Try it on,' Angelo urged. 'It matches your eyes.'

Still unsure, she took the dress from him and went back to the sumptuous dressing room, complete with a chaise and three-panelled cheval mirror.

'Would you like any help?' the sales clerk, a tall, blonde woman with cold eyes and spike heels, asked. She'd been gushing all over them ever since Angelo had entered, acting as if he owned the place, but Lucia had a feeling the assistant wasn't fooled by her.

'I'm fine, thank you,' she said, and closed the door.

She knew she should be gratified by such attention, thrilled by Angelo's wealth and power. Surely most women would be, and she suspected he wanted her to be. Yet while she was proud of what he accomplished, all of it still gave her a sick feeling inside.

Sometimes she felt as if she didn't know this man of power and prestige who had the world at his feet. She didn't know how she could fit into his world...how he could love her.

Resolutely she pushed such pointless worries away, at least for the moment, and slipped into the dress, the silk sliding over with a luxuriant whisper. Angelo rapped on the door.

'Let me see.'

'Give me a minute.' With some wriggling she managed to zip up the back, and with a nervous flutter inside she opened the door. Angelo's pupils flared as he took in the fitted sheath dress ending just below her knee. It was simple, elegant, clearly expensive.

'*Magnifico*. We'll take it.'

'Don't you want to ask if I like it?'

His eyes widened with surprise. 'Don't you?'

She sighed, chuckled in defeat. 'Yes, I do.'

'Then there is no problem.'

'No,' she agreed. 'No problem.'

And there really wasn't. Why couldn't she just relax and enjoy all of this, allow herself to be swept along on this luxurious ride? Everything in her resisted it, resisted not just accepting Angelo's gifts, but acknowledging who he was, powerful, wealthy, entitled. She didn't want him to change her, but she didn't want him to be changed either. And she was afraid he already was, afraid Angelo would never be able to love her as she was.

It was an impossible conundrum. *They* were impossible.

Angelo must have sensed some of what she was feeling, for as they left the boutique and strolled down the glamorous Via Liberta, he said, 'You're not happy I bought you the dress.'

'I wouldn't say that,' she hedged, and he laughed dryly.

'You'd rather I hadn't, then.'

She grimaced. 'I don't mean to be ungrateful.'

'But you are.' He sounded amused, but underneath the humour she heard hurt.

'I don't need you to buy me things, Angelo,' she said after a moment, and he glanced away.

'What if I need to buy them for you?' he asked quietly. 'I want to buy them, at least. I want to give you things.'

Lucia stopped on the pavement and turned to face him. 'Why?' she asked, and he shrugged impatiently.

'Why not? I think it is a normal thing to want to do.' His voice was sharp in self-defence. 'I want to see you wearing beautiful things. I want to be the one to give them to you.'

It was, Lucia suspected, a way for him to show her he cared. Perhaps the only way he knew how. And if so, she should surely accept it, be glad for it. Yet still she resisted.

'Here's a question,' Angelo said as they continued walking down the street. 'Why don't you want me to give you things? Because I'm not sure I understand that.'

She didn't answer for a long moment. 'I suppose it reminds me of how different we are now,' she finally said slowly. 'How different you are, Angelo.'

He gave her a sideways glance, his rueful smile somehow sad. 'Do you really think I'm that different? Because from the moment I've been back in Sicily I've felt exactly the same.' He drew a shaky breath, his voice low. 'A ragged boy with a bloody nose and broken dreams.' He shook his head as if to dismiss the admission, and Lucia's heart twisted inside her. Didn't he know that was the boy she'd fallen in love with, not the man he seemed determined to be now, wealthy and powerful, striding through life with arrogant determination?

She opened her mouth to tell him as much, but he was already turning into another shop, this one even more exclusive and expensive-looking, with black velvet cases and diamonds winking in the window.

'Angelo—' she said, his name a warning, and he shook his head.

'You need something to go with the dress. If it makes

you feel better, you can return to me anything I buy after.'

After? After the Corretti Cup, or after he was finished with her? She knew she shouldn't be thinking that way, and yet she couldn't keep the thoughts from slipping into her mind, sly and insidious. As much as she wanted to, she didn't yet believe this could last. Perhaps that was why she refused his gifts. She was trying to protect herself, paltry attempt that it was, because she didn't trust him to love her, not to leave her.

'Try this.'

While her thoughts had been tangling themselves into knots Angelo had spoken to another snooty shop assistant who had brought out a gorgeous diamond necklace, a dozen glittering square-cut diamonds, each one encrusted with a dozen smaller ones. The thing was intricate, ornate and clearly the most expensive item in the shop.

Lucia shook her head.

'Just try it on,' Angelo persisted, and silently she allowed him to fasten the piece around her neck. The stones felt cold and sharp against the fragile skin of her throat, heavy on her neck.

Angelo's mouth curved in a smile of primal possession. *'Bellissima,'* he said in satisfaction, and she shook her head again.

'It's too much, Angelo.' Wordlessly she unclasped the necklace and handed it back to him. 'I'd look ridiculous in it.' Angelo frowned. She was still trying to distance herself, she knew, still acting out of fear and self-protection, yet she wanted to try. Trust could be a choice. Sometimes it had to be.

She took a deep breath and scanned the display cases. 'How about that?' She pointed to a whimsical dragonfly hair clip, its wings winking with diamonds and sapphires.

Angelo's frown deepened. 'You'd rather have that?'

She'd rather have nothing, rather have Angelo as the boy she knew and loved rather than this autocratic man who insisted on draping her in diamonds, yet she could hardly articulate that to him now. 'Yes.'

He gestured to the shop assistant, who took it out of the case. Lucia slid it into her hair, and was gratified to see Angelo's hard features soften into a smile. He nodded to the assistant. 'We'll take it.'

After they left the jewellery boutique they wandered along the waterfront and then into a restaurant that had, Angelo told her, the freshest seafood on all of Sicily.

The mood between them had lightened again, and Lucia revelled in the ease and enjoyment they had in each other's company. When Angelo was being himself.

'The neighbourhood could use some improvement,' she joked as they went inside, for while the restaurant was top drawer it was surrounded by unused docks and abandoned warehouses.

'The government is planning to regenerate this area,' he told her as they sipped chilled white wine on a terrace overlooking the harbour. 'Actually, I'm part of the process. I've secured a bid to redevelop a housing estate in the area.'

'You have?'

He smiled, his eyes crinkling at the corners and flashing grey-green. 'Don't sound so surprised.'

'I didn't realise you had so much business in Sicily.' He shrugged, averting his gaze, and Lucia couldn't keep from adding, 'But you never intend to live here.'

'Not permanently, no.'

She nodded, accepting, even as she wondered if he

simply didn't see that as a problem for their fledgling relationship. Admittedly, there wasn't too much to keep her in Sicily any more. Her mother was dead, her father long gone, and what few friends she had weren't particularly close ones. And yet…

Again, she resisted. Resisted giving more to this man, because she was still bracing herself for the moment when he decided he'd had enough. When he walked away…again.

Firmly she pushed that thought away. She needed to try. *Trust was a choice.* 'What made you decide to come back to Sicily after all this time? Just the business opportunity?'

Angelo's gaze rested on her for a moment, narrowed, shuttered. Then he smiled and took a sip of wine. 'Yes,' he answered. 'Just business.'

They walked along the waterfront for a while after lunch, and then back into the old quarter of the city. The sun was hot overhead and it was pleasant to wander hand in hand through the narrow streets with their crumbling buildings and open-air markets. Despite the elegant, expensive clothes and the pervasive aura of wealth, Angelo seemed like the boy she remembered. The boy she loved.

'This almost feels like old times,' she said, only half teasing.

'Doesn't it?' He turned to her with a smile, although she still sensed that guarded sorrow shadowing his eyes, tensing the lines around his mouth. 'I think you're the only person I've ever been myself with.' The admission, so quietly made, rocked her, because it was so achingly honest—and because she felt the same. Hope bloomed within once more, more powerful than ever.

'Me too,' she said quietly, and squeezed his hand. 'Me too.'

* * *

Angelo couldn't remember when he'd enjoyed a day more. For a whole day spent in Lucia's company he'd felt the tightness inside him ease, the emptiness fill. He felt happy. He felt whole.

The realisation terrified him.

He'd told Lucia love was complicated, messy, and it was. He felt it in all of its uncontainable sprawl now, disordering his thoughts, his ambitions, everything. He'd come to Sicily with a simple plan: to ruin the Correttis. Revenge, simple and sweet, served twenty years' cold. He'd convinced himself it was all he wanted, and yet now…?

Now he wanted this. Her. And not just her, but a life with her, a life he'd never, ever imagined having or even wanting. A life he still could bear to think about only in vague images: a house somewhere, a kitchen with sunlight and a bowl of fruit on the table. A child toddling towards him and loving arms slipping around his waist.

Even those images felt impossibly remote, like fuzzy photographs of another planet. A place he'd never been, and wasn't sure he could go.

A place he wasn't sure he *should* go.

'Angelo?' Lucia turned to him with a smile, although he saw the worry clouding her eyes. Always the worry, the fear. He felt it too.

'I should take you back home,' he said. 'I need to get back to work.'

'I see.'

And she probably did see, all too much. He hadn't meant it as a brush-off precisely, but it served as one. It was time to get back to the reason why he'd come back to Sicily at all. It was time to focus on what really mattered.

They didn't speak as he drove her back to Caltarione. As soon as they hit the narrow, dusty streets of the village that time itself seemed to have forgotten he felt himself tense. Resist. He hated this place, hated the memories that came up inside him like the clouds of dust on the road, obscuring everything.

Just like he'd told Lucia, he couldn't escape that old feeling. Here he was once again that foolish boy, ragged and angry, whom everybody had ignored or dismissed. He felt the frustration boil up inside him along with the determination to not be that boy again. Lucia didn't seem to want him to be different, but he needed to be. Needed to be someone who would stand up to the Correttis, who would *count*—

'Stop here,' Lucia said softly, and he glanced at her in surprise for they were still at the top end of the village's main street, at least a quarter of a mile from her house. Then he saw they were outside the church, and realisation slammed into his chest, rocked him to the core.

'Are you sure?'

She nodded, and he parked the car on the kerb. The air was dry and still as they climbed out of the car, and although he couldn't see a single person on the narrow, winding street, he could feel the prying eyes, the pursed lips. How many people were peering out at them from behind latticed shutters, recognising him as the Corretti bastard they'd once ignored and reviled?

And how many people recognised Lucia as the woman who had borne his child, people who would never see her as anything else?

Dio, he wanted so much more for her. He wanted to give it to her. Why couldn't she understand that? Accept it?

He turned to her now, saw her face was pale and set. Before last night he'd never considered what life must have been like for her after he'd left. She would have been pregnant, unwed, alone. In a tiny place like Caltarione life must have been intolerable. His throat thickened and at first words wouldn't come.

'I'm sorry,' he said, and she turned to stare at him.

'What for?'

He saw the wariness enter her eyes, her body tensing in expectation. Afraid—of what? That he would let her down now, already? 'For not being here when you were pregnant. And, I suppose, for not even thinking about how hard it must have been for you in a place like this. Not until you told me.' She shrugged and he asked quietly, 'Was it very hard?'

'It was worth it.'

'Even though—'

'Yes,' she cut him off with a quiet certainty. 'Even though.'

He felt the thickness in his throat again, the moisture in his eyes. What was happening to him? How had he become this weak wreck of a man, devastated by emotion?

'Let's go,' Lucia said, and she took his hand, her own hand cold in his. Silently she led him around the side of the church and into the cemetery behind, past the older headstones now weathered and worn, some toppled over, to a small garden in the back built into the hillside with just a few small headstones. And there, in the corner, a small rectangle of white marble commemorated his child.

Angelo stared at the few, heartbreakingly simple words. *Angelica. Molto amata.* Much loved.

He reached out and laid one hand on the marble headstone; it was warm from the sun. He felt tears again, harder this time to ignore. He couldn't speak; he was slain by weakness. He should have been here. He should have been here for Angelica, for *Lucia*.

Then he felt her arm slide around his waist and she laid her head on his shoulder, her touch like a healing balm. He took a shuddering breath.

'I'm sorry,' he said again.

'I know,' Lucia answered softly. 'But I didn't bring you here to open up the wounds of the past, Angelo. I brought you here to heal them. To look towards the future.' She spoke tremulously; he felt her uncertainty.

The future. The future scared him, and he suspected it scared her too. What could a future with Lucia look like? A future with love in it, a life he was afraid of because he didn't really believe it could ever be his? It never had been before.

The sun had started to sink behind the church and the cemetery was lost in shadows. Angelo turned away from his daughter's grave.

'We should go,' he said, and silently Lucia followed him back to the car.

An hour later, having dropped her off at her apartment, Angelo strode into his office above the Corretti Hotel. He felt restless, edgy, unfulfilled. The afternoon with Lucia had opened up old wounds, new doubts. He craved being with her, even as he hated the weakness of that craving. The need it showed in him, a need that could surely never be filled.

All you were meant to be was a stain on the sheets.

His father's sneering voice.

You were a mistake, Angelo. It would have been better if you'd never lived.

His grandparents, sighing with weary defeat.

I'm sorry. I should never have had you.

His mother, ashamed and defiant.

No one had wanted him. No one had loved him. He'd learned to live without love, had trained himself not to want it. And now Lucia came once more into his life, with her hope and her love and her *fear*.

He knew she was afraid he would let her down, no matter what she said. He knew it because he felt it too. Wouldn't it be easier for everyone if he just stopped now? Admitted it couldn't work, it wasn't in him? Wouldn't it save them both a lot of heartbreak? And God only knew Lucia had had enough, with his own abandonment and the death of their daughter—

'Signor Corretti? There have been messages....'

Yanked from his thoughts, Angelo glanced impatiently at his receptionist, a woman who had worked for the Correttis and whom he hadn't had time to replace, as she half rose from behind her desk.

'Leave them on my desk.'

He stalked into his office, felt the beginnings of another migraine pulse at his temples. He snatched the scrawled messages on his desk and scanned them, the pain at his temples pulsing harder as he realised what this day had cost him.

A message from one of Corretti Designs' shareholders, the banker from Milan who was having second thoughts about Luca remaining as CEO. Another message from Battaglia, wanting to speak to him about the regeneration bid. A message from Alessandro Corretti, his unacknowledged half-brother, who wanted to set up a meeting about that same bid.

Angelo dropped the sheaf of messages. One damned day might have set back all his plans. Who even knew what opportunities he'd missed while he'd been dallying with Lucia, chasing dreams he had no right to harbour, not even for a moment?

Dio, he'd been so stupid. So *weak*.

Resolutely he sat down at his desk and pulled the phone towards him. Any thoughts of Lucia, of love, had deserted him completely, replaced only by cold, hard purpose. This was why he was here. This was what he had come for.

Lucia gazed at her reflection. The dragonfly clip sparkled in her hair, which she'd styled into loose waves. The sapphire blue of the dress glowed against her skin. She wore cheap shoes.

Funny, but Angelo hadn't thought of that. Neither had she. Dress, check. Jewelry, check. Shoes? A pair of scuffed pumps she'd had for nearly a decade. And as for her underwear…if they ever got that far, Angelo would encounter plain white cotton that had definitely seen better days.

Sighing, she turned away from the mirror.

She wasn't even sure if any of it mattered. It had been five days since Angelo had dropped her off after their day together, and she hadn't seen him at all. Hadn't received so much as a phone call or text message or note. This was all starting to seem horribly familiar. The hope, the dread, the silence.

They hadn't even lasted a week.

Stop it, she told herself. He'd been busy, of course he had. He was an important man, with important deals to make. She understood that, even if she didn't like it. Trust was a choice.

Taking a deep breath, she went into the living room to wait for Angelo. His assistant had sent a message earlier that day that he would pick her up at five. Well, here she was. She only hoped he hadn't changed his mind… about anything. *About everything.*

At ten minutes past five Lucia started to worry. At quarter past, she began to doubt. And at half past, she felt horribly resigned—and that was when she heard quick footsteps on the stairs and a sharp rap at the door.

She opened the door, saw Angelo's gaze sweep over her quickly before he looked away. 'I'm sorry I'm late.'

She nodded, accepting his terse apology even as questions clamoured in her throat. 'What happened?' she asked, keeping her voice light, mild, and Angelo just shrugged.

'A business meeting ran late. Shall we?' He held out his arm and after a moment's pause Lucia slipped her hand through it. She could feel the tension vibrating through Angelo's arm, his whole body. Something had happened. Something was wrong.

That old fear lurched inside her, and she almost pulled away. Almost turned around and went straight back into her apartment. She didn't want this, hated the sense of clingy desperation that flooded through her, just as it must have flooded through her mother. Justify. Excuse. Appease. And all to keep a man around.

Trust is a choice.

'Is something wrong, Angelo?' she asked evenly, and he glanced back at her, his expression sharp and almost hostile until, with effort, he smoothed it out.

'No, I'm sorry. I've been a bit…stressed about work. That's all.' He drew her to him, kissed the top of her head. She slid her arms around him, pressed her cheek against his chest so she could feel the thud of his heart. She felt something in him loosen, relax. He sighed softly. 'You look amazing, you know, and utterly beautiful.'

She felt herself relax too, then. She didn't need to be so suspicious and uneasy. She had to stop waiting, expecting Angelo to let her down. She leaned back to smile at him. 'You look pretty amazing too.'

'And beautiful?' Angelo said with a quirk of his eyebrow, a faint smile on his lips.

'Actually, yes.' Because he was a beautiful man. Long lashes, full lips, high cheekbones. A woman would kill for all of those, and yet Angelo possessed them in an utterly masculine way.

'Let's go,' he said, and linking his hand in hers, he led her downstairs to the Porsche.

They didn't talk too much as they drove along the coast to the racetrack that held the Corretti Cup. Angelo made a few attempts at small talk, but Lucia could tell he was preoccupied—the tension stealing through him again, his fingers tapping the steering wheel—and she wondered how he felt about attending such a prestigious event, hosted by his cousin. Did he still hate his Corretti relations, even as he defiantly bore their name? It was yet another one of his integral contradictions: the ragged boy, the regal businessman. The Corretti who both hated and claimed his name.

As Angelo drove up to the front of the racetrack, a valet came around for the car, and another opened her door. Lucia stepped out, saw an array of women dressed head-to-toe in designer outfits, sleek and privileged and looking world-weary, while she had her pretty dress, her dragonfly hair clip and her cheap, old shoes.

She swallowed dryly, grateful for Angelo's steadying presence as he came beside her, slid his arm through hers.

'What's the schedule of events?' she asked as they joined the decked-out throng streaming towards the main entrance of the track. Angelo sidestepped the crowd and headed towards a separate door marked VIP Only. A dark-suited man allowed them to pass without so much as a blink.

You should be thrilled, Lucia told herself. *VIP!* But she only felt outclassed and uneasy.

'The main race is first,' Angelo said, his arm around her shoulders as he guided her down a private corridor to an even more private box of seats. Lucia sat down on a plush chair, watched as a waiter poured them both champagne. 'And then a champagne reception afterwards.'

'More champagne,' Lucia said as she accepted the crystal flute. 'I've never even had champagne before, you know.'

Angelo smiled faintly. 'See if you like it.'

She didn't. The taste was crisp and tart on her tongue, not sweet at all, and the bubbles went up her nose. She put her glass down on the marble-topped table between them and resisted the urge to wipe her damp palms down the sides of her dress.

She didn't like being here. She didn't like being here with Angelo, who was scanning the different boxes with narrowed eyes, his lips thinned, looking both powerful and predatory.

'Are you going to place a bet?' she asked, and he gave her a quick glance and nod.

'Oh, yes.'

There was something about his grimly certain tone that made her feel even more uneasy. 'Which horse?'

Angelo paused, then answered crisply, 'Cry of Thunder to win.'

Lucia didn't know a thing about horse racing, but from hearing the chatter and gossip in the staff room, she did know that Cry of Thunder was an upstart contender from Spain, a horse that no one was backing because of course everyone wanted Gio Corretti's Sicilian-bred horse to win.

Everyone except Angelo.

'Cry of Thunder?' she repeated after a moment. 'He's not likely to win, is he?'

Angelo hesitated for only a second. 'No.'

'So why are you betting on him, then?'

He shifted in his seat. 'There are more important things than money.'

'Of course there are.' Angelo's tone had been repressive, but Lucia couldn't ignore the deepening unease she felt, prickling along her spine and souring her stomach. 'But a horserace…betting, gambling…that's about money, surely? About winning?'

Angelo glanced at her, and his expression was completely unreadable. All the emotion and need, the hope and happiness, she'd once seen in his eyes was veiled, masked. His eyes were flat and dark, the colour of moss on stone. 'It's definitely about winning,' he finally said, which was no answer at all.

A few other guests entered the VIP box then, and Angelo stood as he said hello to several expensive-suited corporate types. Lucia saw one of the women, a sleek brunette, flick a dismissive glance first towards her frivolous hair clip and then at her shoes. She fought not to blush. Damn her shoes anyway. If she'd been trying to fool anybody, she obviously wasn't. Everyone could see how she didn't belong here.

And she *wasn't* trying to fool anybody, Lucia reminded herself fiercely. This was not her world. She didn't want it to be Angelo's world. She wanted to go home.

'All right?' Angelo asked, and reached for the champagne bottle to top up her barely touched flute.

'Yes.' Lucia smiled tightly. Every muscle in her body ached with tension, and the evening had barely started. She glanced at Angelo, who was leaning forward, his body looking as tense as hers felt. He wasn't enjoying himself either, she thought suddenly, and she felt a flicker of something almost like relief. Maybe they weren't so different at all. Neither of them wanted to be here.

They didn't talk much as more people took their seats and then the race started. Lucia watched the horses, elegantly sinuous, eat up the track, clouds of dust billowing behind them and the sea a sunlit shimmer on the horizon. She couldn't tell what was going on, but it was over soon enough—and Cry of Thunder had come in fifth. Gio Corretti's horse had won.

'How much did you lose?' she asked, smiling, trying to keep it light, and Angelo shrugged.

'It doesn't matter.'

After the race they went with the other VIPs into a glittering ballroom. Tuxedoed waiters passed around yet more champagne as well as chocolate-dipped strawberries, caviar, pâté. Food Lucia had never had before and didn't really like, although she helped herself to several strawberries. Angelo kept surveying the ballroom, his eyes narrowed as if he were looking for someone. He barely spoke to Lucia, and her unease turned to pure feminine annoyance.

'Angelo—'

'Come here.' He took her elbow, striding forward towards a man Lucia recognised from earlier, Gio Corretti—a son of Benito Corretti, a cousin of Angelo's.

The man inclined his head slightly in cool acknowledgement and Angelo smiled back, although there was no friendliness or warmth in that curving of lips. He looked hard, unyielding, ruthless. Underneath her hand his arm felt as if it had been hewn from granite, forged from steel.

'You lost quite a bit tonight,' Gio remarked as he shook Angelo's outstretched hand. Angelo's smile deepened, became even colder.

'Pocket change, Gio.'

'Ah.' Gio Corretti nodded slowly. 'I see.'

Lucia didn't see anything at all. The men stared at each other, Angelo cold, Gio chillingly remote. Lucia felt like screaming at them to behave—but of course, to all intents and purposes, they were behaving. No fisticuffs, no hurling of insults. Just this cold, hard, glittering anger. Like the diamonds Angelo had wanted to buy for her, costly and soulless.

'I'm not the one you're fighting, you know,' Gio said quietly, and Angelo's whole body stiffened as if he'd been jerked on a string.

'Who said I'm fighting?'

'Aren't you?'

'It's business.'

'Some business.' Gio shrugged, turned away, and Angelo stood there, his whole body quivering with tension, with anger. *With hurt.*

Lucia could feel it coming off him in waves, knew he felt like he'd been dismissed, rejected by a Corretti. What she saw in Gio Corretti was a grudging respect for a self-made man like Angelo, but Angelo hadn't seen it.

'Angelo…' she murmured, and he shook his head, shrugged off her arm.

'Let's go.'

As relieved as she was to get out of there, she didn't like the way he seemed about to stomp off, pulling her along with him. 'Don't you think—'

'I've done what I came to do,' Angelo said flatly,

and reaching for her hand, he led her swiftly out of the ballroom.

They didn't talk until they were in the Porsche, speeding back towards Palermo, the night inky-black all around them.

'What was that all about?' Lucia asked quietly.

'What do you mean?'

'Why did you bring me there, Angelo? Why did you go yourself?' She shook her head, bewildered, uncertain, starting to get angry. 'You certainly didn't go because you enjoyed the experience.'

'Did you?' Angelo tossed back, and she leaned her head back against the seat.

'No, not at all. But does that really surprise you? I've never—' She stopped suddenly, and Angelo glanced at her with narrowed, knowing eyes.

'You've never what?' he prompted softly.

'I've never wanted to be in that kind of crowd,' she finished, choosing her words with care. 'Have that kind of life.'

Angelo arched an incredulous eyebrow. 'You've never,' he stated disbelievingly, 'wanted more out of life than making other people's beds, cleaning their damn toilets—'

'It's a job, Angelo. It's respectable, it pays—'

'There's more to life than a *job*.'

'Oh, yes, there is. There's love and family and children and happiness.' Her throat clogged and her chest hurt. She didn't know how they'd got into this argument, but she had a gut instinct that the only way to get out was to wade through. She swallowed hard. 'But I don't think you meant those kinds of things.'

'No, I didn't.' Angelo stared straight ahead, flexed his fingers on the wheel. The night-shrouded landscape

passed by in a blur of black. Lucia closed her eyes. She
didn't like where this conversation was going. He didn't
say anything else, and she thought they might spend the
entire journey back to Palermo in this stony silence. A
question burned in her gut, churned its way up her throat.

'How much money did you lose?'

'Does it matter?'

'I think it does.'

Angelo threw her a quick, irritated glance. 'Why? I
have plenty. And you don't even like me to spend it on
you, so—'

'It's not about the money.'

'What, then?'

She shook her head wearily. 'Perhaps you should tell
me that.'

'Stop talking in riddles, Lucia—'

'Then you stop putting me off,' she retorted. 'You
didn't bring me to the Corretti Cup as a date, did you,
Angelo? You didn't even buy me that dress or want to
buy me those ridiculous diamonds because you wanted
to please me or make me happy.' It was all becoming horribly clear, like wiping the steam from a mirror. Slowly,
surely, she could see the whole, awful reflection.

'Why do you think I did, then?' Angelo asked in a
colourless voice.

'Because you wanted to show me off. Show yourself
off.' Lucia spoke mechanically; she felt weirdly lifeless,
almost as if she didn't care about it any more. 'You went
to the Corretti Cup to thumb your nose at all the Correttis you still hate, even though it's been fifteen years since
you left. Even though you probably have more money
than they do now. That's why you bet on the losing horse,
isn't it? Just to show you could lose however much money
and it didn't matter.' More mist cleared; the reflection

sharpened. 'And that's why you bought the hotel.' The realisation lay heavily within her. 'What are you trying to do, Angelo? Ruin them?'

'Anything that happens to them, they deserve.'

'They *deserve*? Does anyone deserve to be ruined? Why are you even angry at them, Angelo? It's your father you're really angry at and he's—'

'Don't,' he said in a low voice, 'talk about my father.'

'Why not?'

He let out a low breath and shook his head. 'I just don't want to talk about him.'

Lucia sat back against her seat and closed her eyes. She felt utterly drained, her mind numb and empty. She should have thought about this, she realised dully. She should have expected this. She remembered how angry and bitter Angelo had been as a child; had she thought he'd changed?

That was why she didn't like all this power and wealth, she knew now. It really wasn't about the money. It was about the reason, the motivation. The revenge. The hard core of bitterness and anger Angelo would never relinquish. How could love flourish in such a heart? How could it even survive?

They'd reached Caltarione, and Angelo pulled up in front of her apartment. Tinny music and raucous laughter spilled out from the bar beneath. Lucia opened her eyes and saw Angelo staring straight ahead, his jaw bunched, his body tense.

'I don't even see why any of it matters,' he said flatly. 'It has nothing to do with us.' Lucia just shook her head. She didn't know how even to begin to explain. 'Why does it bother you?' he demanded, his voice harsh now. 'It's not as if any of the Correttis have ever done you a good turn, Lucia. Or as if you cared about them—did

you?' His voice hardened in suspicion, and Lucia turned
to him slowly.

'What are you saying?' she asked in a low voice.

'Why are you so defensive of the Correttis?' Angelo
challenged. 'Did one of my half-brothers offer some
comfort while I was away—maybe you wanted to be
with a *real* Corretti—'

Lucia didn't think. She just reacted, reaching out and
slapping Angelo hard across the face. He blinked, and
she watched an angry red handprint bloom across his
cheek.

He reached up with one hand and touched his cheek,
his expression one of cold disbelief. Lucia held her
breath. She didn't regret slapping him, not one bit, but
she regretted everything else. This whole evening. This
argument. The man he'd become.

Angelo held his hand up to his cheek, his expression
coldly remote, and Lucia stared back, her chest heaving.
Then his face crumpled and he covered it with both his
hands as he let out a shuddering breath.

'*Dio*, I'm sorry,' he said, the words coming out on
a half-groan. 'How could I say such a thing to you? I
didn't believe it for a moment.' He dropped his hands and
looked at her with such aching bleakness that Lucia suddenly felt near tears herself. 'Forgive me, Lucia. Forgive
me for everything. I'm such a bastard—a true bastard,
and not just one by birth. I've treated you terribly. I always have.' He drew in a ragged breath. 'I can't do this.'

She reached out and cupped his cheek, the one still
red from her slap. 'You *are* doing it, Angelo. Just saying
that is more than you've ever done before.'

He grimaced. 'That's not saying very much.'

'Still.' She tried to smile. 'It's something.'

Angelo stared at her, his eyes glittering, his chest

heaving with ragged breaths. 'Let's get out of here,' he said suddenly. 'Out of Sicily. Being back here—it makes me someone I don't want to be. Let me take you some-where, Lucia—somewhere you've never been, away from all of this. Just for a little while.'

'But my—' She stopped, because she could not mis-take the desperation in Angelo's voice. She knew, in her own way, she'd been as stubborn as he was, refusing his gifts, refusing to change or even give an inch of her life over to this man. But maybe now they both needed compromise. Escape.

'Please, Lucia.'

She smiled again and slowly leaned forward to kiss his lips. 'Yes,' she answered. 'Let's escape.'

CHAPTER ELEVEN

ANGELO GAZED AT Lucia sitting across from him in his private jet and smiled. He'd made the right decision, leaving Sicily for a little while. Escaping, just as Lucia had said. He'd hated how he felt there, trapped as the boy he'd once been, determined to prove himself yet still dismissed.

He remembered how Gio Corretti had turned away from him, indifferent, dismissive, and his heart burned inside him. Perhaps Gio would think differently when he took over another chunk of Corretti Enterprises. Last night, after he'd left Lucia, he'd put several meetings into place with various shareholders in Corretti Enterprises's different interests. He might have to wait on Corretti Designs, but other companies under the Corretti umbrella were ripe for the taking. And he intended to take.

'You're frowning,' Lucia said quietly, and he returned his distant gaze to her, taking in the blueness of her eyes, shadowed grey by a moment's worry. She didn't understand, Angelo knew. Didn't share his need to equal the Correttis, to rise above them.

'Sorry, I was lost in thought.' He leaned forward to brush his lips against hers, all his plans for meetings and takeovers momentarily forgotten as her mouth met his. She tasted so unbearably sweet, and he longed to take her in his arms, to lose himself in her generous warmth.

They'd hadn't done more than kiss since that unforgettable, tempestuous night at his villa. He hoped that might
change today. Tonight.

'So you haven't even told me where we're going,'
Lucia said, and Angelo was gratified to see her eyes
clear to sapphire. 'Not too far away, I hope.'

'No.' He glanced out the window and smiled. 'We're
almost there.'

Twenty minutes later the jet touched down. As she
stepped out onto the tarmac Lucia clutched her hands
together, turned to Angelo with shining eyes. 'Paris.'

'You always said you wanted to go.'

'I did, didn't I?'

He drew her towards him, unable to resist kissing her
again. 'I hope it lives up to your expectations.'

'I think it will,' Lucia murmured as she kissed him
back.

Angelo felt his insides lift, lighten. Coming here had
been such a good idea. Here, away from Sicily, their
childhoods, the memories and prejudices, they could be
themselves…and learn to love each other all over again.

Lucia felt as if she were floating. She was finally in
Paris—and with Angelo. It was her birthday and Christ-
mas all in one, everything she'd ever wanted. Almost.

They rode a limo into the city, and Lucia kept her nose
nearly pressed to the glass as she watched the monu-
ments flash by: le Place de Concorde, l'Arc de Triom-
phe, the huge Louvre with its winking glass pyramids
and of course the Eiffel Tower, a glorious steel pinnacle
piercing the sky. She had a postcard of each one, but the
reality, even from behind the tinted window of a limo,
was far better.

'I want to see it *all*,' she breathed, and Angelo chuckled.

'And you will. But first let's check in and get something to eat.'

They checked into the Presidential Suite at the Georges Cinq Hotel, and after the bellhop had left Lucia walked around slowly, taking in the antiques, the huge marble bathtub, the private terrace. She'd cleaned such rooms, of course, working at the hotel, but she'd never stayed in one before.

She stared out at the City of Light dazzled by a noonday sun and shook her head in wonder.

'Do you like it?' Angelo asked, and to her own shame she heard an uncertain note of vulnerability in his voice.

'Do I like it?' she repeated, and turned around. 'It's the most amazing place I've ever been. It's even better than the penthouse suite at the Corretti!'

He chuckled softly. 'For now. I intend to make the Corretti the most luxurious hotel in all of Europe.'

'And you'll manage that easily, I'm sure.' Away from Sicily, from the memories and prejudices, she felt her resistance to Angelo's wealth melt away. He was a different man here, and she was a different woman. Finally they could be the people they wanted to be, the people they were meant to be, loving each other.

She walked towards him, reached for his hands. 'Thank you for bringing me here, Angelo.'

She felt his tension ease, saw his countenance lighten. 'Thank you for coming.' He drew her towards him and she came willingly. 'I'm glad we escaped.'

He slid his arms around her and she pressed her cheek against his chest, felt the reassuring thud of his heart. 'It felt like a close one,' she whispered, and his arms tightened around her.

'I know.'

She didn't say anything more, didn't want to drag

them both down into argument once again. They had time to work out their differences, time to change and heal. 'Let's go see the city,' she said instead, and he laughed ruefully, his arms still around her.

'I have some good ideas of what we could do right here, you know.'

Her heart seemed to turn right over, her insides tightening with longing. She had a good idea too, and if it actually came down to a choice between seeing the Eiffel Tower and making love with Angelo…well, the postcard really was a good likeness, wasn't it? Although the thought of actually making love with Angelo—not just a moment's grasped pleasure, a one-night stand—thrilled her and terrified her in equal parts. It would be so much *more*.

Still chuckling, Angelo released her. 'Come on. I couldn't live with myself if I didn't let you see the Eiffel Tower.'

It was better than the postcard, Lucia decided as they took the lift to the top viewing level. The city lay spread before them in a living map, the sky cloudless and blue above. Angelo slipped his hand in hers as they stared out at the endless view.

'Is it as you imagined?'

'Better.'

'It's nice when things live up to your expectations,' he said dryly.

Some strange impulse made her ask, 'Has this lived up to your expectations, Angelo?'

'This?' he repeated, his voice turning just a little guarded and Lucia gazed at him openly, wanting, even needing, this honesty between them.

She wasn't really sure what she was asking. 'Success,' she said after a pause. 'Wealth. Power. Revenge, even—all of it. Has it lived up to your expectations? Is it everything you hoped it would be?'

Angelo squinted as he gazed out at the city. 'Wealth and power have their advantages.'

'But do they fill that emptiness inside?'

She felt him tense, saw his eyes narrow and his pupils flare. 'What are you talking about?'

'Do you remember?' she asked softly. 'When your— when Carlo Corretti died, and you came and found me. Do you remember what you said?'

She could tell by the way his mouth tightened and he looked away that he did. *He'd dead, Lucia, and I don't feel anything. I just feel empty.*

'Why are we talking about this?' Angelo asked, his tone even and yet also edged with impatience, annoyance. 'I thought we came to Paris to forget about all that, at least for a little while.'

'Is it wrong of me to want to know? To want to know you?'

He let out a sigh. 'Not wrong. Just…difficult. We'll argue about it, Lucia. I know that. You don't see things the way I do.' A fair point, yet she knew the implication was that he was seeing things correctly and she wasn't.

Lucia decided to leave it. Why ruin a perfect afternoon by insisting on a discussion she wasn't sure either of them were ready to have?

'We don't have to talk about it now,' she said quietly, and with a grateful smile Angelo turned from the railing.

'There's plenty more to see in this city, you know.'

They spent the afternoon touring the sights, taking in the endless steps of Montmartre and the quaint, narrow streets of the Latin Quarter, the modern Centre Pompidou and the ancient Louvre.

They wandered down the Champs-élysées and Angelo

insisted on buying her a dress for dinner, a strappy black number that made Lucia feel both sophisticated and sexy.

'And we'd better not forget the shoes,' he murmured, his eyes glinting, and she laughed, realising he'd noticed her old shoes from before. 'How about these?' He'd stopped in front of an exclusive-looking boutique and pointed to a pair of diamante-encrusted stilettos. The heel was at least five inches high.

'They're ridiculous,' she protested.

'True,' Angelo agreed solemnly. 'But you do love them.'

Lucia had to admit that she did. She'd never possessed anything frivolous or extravagant before, and suddenly those silvery stilettos seemed the best shoes in the world.

Angelo led her by the hand into the boutique, and a few minutes later he was slipping one of the stilettos onto her foot.

'I feel like Cinderella,' she said with a laugh, and he glanced up at her with passion-darkened eyes.

'You're my Cinderella.'

'That's the only one I want to be.' She swallowed, her heart suddenly starting to pound, and then stood. She felt about ten feet tall in the heels, and she tottered around the shop, feeling outrageous and yet so very sexy.

'We'll take them,' Angelo told the sales assistant. He pulled Lucia close so only she could hear his whispered words. 'I have a fantasy of seeing you wearing those and nothing else.'

A blush fired Lucia's body and she glanced away. 'That sounds like a…an interesting fantasy,' she murmured.

By the time they'd arrived back at the hotel Lucia was exhausted but also happy. All afternoon Angelo had been relaxed, fun, even silly. He'd been the boy she had missed, the boy she'd fallen in love with. Underneath the hard gloss of wealth and power he was still there, and the realisation made her heart sing with joy.

As she walked into the suite, still amazed by the sheer luxuriousness of the place, she stopped suddenly for the doors to the private terrace were ajar, and she could see a table there, laid with linen and flickering with candlelight.

She turned back to Angelo. 'How—?'

'I'd like to say it took great planning and precision, but all it really took was a phone call.'

'Even so,' Lucia murmured, touched more than she could say by his thoughtfulness. She gave a slight grimace, gestured to her plain T-shirt and capris. 'I think I have half the dirt of Paris on me.'

'There's no reason why you can't make good use of that huge marble shower,' Angelo said with a glint in his eyes. 'We both could.'

Lucia's breath caught in her chest as she remembered how they'd made very good use of the shower in Angelo's villa. He laughed softly and shook his head.

'No, there will be time for that later. Bathe and we'll eat first.'

'All right.' She headed for the bathroom, peeled her clothes from her body and stepped under the hot, powerful spray. Why, she wondered as she washed her hair, did Angelo's words feel a bit like a temporary reprieve? She wanted to make love with him, had dreamt of it, and yet…

She was afraid. Afraid that now they were actually trying to have a real relationship, sex might ruin it. She might disappoint him. He might walk away afterwards.

'Stop it,' she said aloud, her words lost in the shower spray. 'Stop waiting for the worst to happen.' She'd lived her life like that for too long already. Now she wanted to hope. To believe.

Trust was a choice.

She wore the strappy black dress Angelo had bought for her earlier, and the silver stilettos. Gazing at her reflection in the mirror, she hardly recognised herself. Her hair tumbled loosely about her shoulders, and her eyes were smoky and dark with anticipation. With passion. As for the dress…it clung to every curve before flaring out about her thighs. The silver stilettos made her legs look endless.

Taking a deep breath, she headed out to the terrace. Angelo was already out there, having showered and changed into a pair of charcoal-grey trousers and a white button-down shirt, open at the throat. His hair curled against his neck and as he turned to her his eyes blazed almost emerald and for a moment Lucia forgot how to breathe.

In, out, lungs filling—she had to tell herself, remind her body of its basic functions because every sense, every cell and neuron, was short-circuited by awareness.

She loved him so much.

'Bellissima,' Angelo said softly as he came towards her. *'Mi cucciola.'* She didn't mind the endearment then, knew it was part of their history, who they were.

He took her hands in his and drew her to the table. 'Good enough to eat,' he said, and Lucia laughed.

'And I'm starving.'

She didn't really remember what they talked about that evening, only how easy and relaxed it seemed. How happy she felt, and how happy she knew Angelo felt; the tautness was gone from his body, the shadows from his eyes.

The City of Light had settled into silence for the evening, the sun streaking its last orange rays across the horizon. As the sky deepened into indigo, Angelo reached for her hand and pointed to the Eiffel Tower.

'Watch.'

The last of the sun's light sank from the sky and the lights of the Eiffel Tower came on, transforming the tower into a diamond-like jewel in the centre of the city, sparkling with lights against a darkening sky.

'*Oh,*' Lucia breathed as she gazed at the lit tower with wonder. 'It's beautiful. I'm so glad I saw it.'

'I'm glad I saw it with you.'

She turned back to Angelo, and saw he was looking at her with heavy-lidded, languorous intent. She swallowed, then whispered, 'Make love to me, Angelo.'

He smiled and drew her up by the hand away from the table, and then from the terrace to the sumptuous bedroom with its huge four-poster bed.

He stood her in front of it, his hands cupping her face. 'You're trembling.'

'I'm…nervous.'

He frowned. 'Why?'

'Because…this is different, isn't it? It should be different. The other times—it was rushed….'

He slid his hands from her face to her shoulders, sliding his fingers through the heavy mass of her hair. 'I don't think it was too rushed in the shower,' he murmured, and she chuckled in acknowledgement, the sound wavering on the still air.

'Yes, I know, but…it still felt temporary. I still thought it was a one-night—'

'This is not for just one night,' Angelo said softly, silencing her words. 'This is the beginning, Lucia, of for ever.' And then he kissed her, softly, his lips brushing across hers, a whisper, a greeting, before her lips parted beneath his and he went deep as her mind went blurry, awash with pleasure.

Slowly, reverently, he slipped the straps of her dress from her shoulders and she stepped out of the garment, wearing only her underwear and the silver heels.

'Ah,' Angelo said as he gazed down at her, drinking her in. 'My fantasy. Almost.' Smiling, he reached forward and undid the clasp of her bra. He slid her panties down her legs and she kicked them off. She was naked, save for the shoes.

And amazingly, she didn't feel embarrassed or uncertain. She felt powerful. Sexy. And incredibly desired. Smiling, she reached for the buttons on his shirt. 'And now it's time for my fantasy.'

Angelo's eyes were dark as he gazed down at her, his voice a husky murmur. 'Which is?'

'You wearing nothing at all.' She slid the shirt from his shoulders and then, fumbling only a little, went for his belt. She drew it through the loops and heard Angelo's breath come out in a hiss as she undid the button of his trousers and then slid them down his legs. His boxers followed and now they were both naked.

Lucia kicked off her shoes. Angelo laughed softly. 'There goes my fantasy.'

'I think I can do better.'

'I'm sure you can. In fact, my fantasy is becoming less and less about shoes and much more about you— and me.' Tugging on her hand, he drew her to the bed, pulling aside the duvet, and then took her into his arms and she curled into him, sliding her legs along his, her softness against the hard, muscular planes of his chest and abdomen. In the comforting cradle of his arms she remembered how good he felt, how *right*. How much she missed this warmth, this connection, and how she never wanted to be without it again.

That connection strengthened with every touch, every kiss, every caress. Lucia arched against him, gasping aloud as he touched her in every intimate place, hands and mouth, fingers and lips. And she touched him back, tentatively at first and then with growing confidence and power, revelling in the way he responded, drawing his breath in a hiss through his teeth as she followed the path blazed by her hands with her mouth. She knew every part of him now, and yet she wanted to know more. Needed more, craved that full union, when her body would be joined with his wholly and utterly.

'Angelo…'

'I'm here, *mi cucciola*,' he whispered as he rolled her onto her back, his body poised over hers. '*Amore mio*. I'm here.' He slid a condom on and then joined his body with hers, filling her right up so she gasped again, her nails biting into his shoulders as she wrapped her legs around his waist and drew him even more fully into herself.

'I—' she gasped, unable to manage more as his body drove her closer and closer to shattering completely. 'I love you—'

'I love you,' Angelo said, his voice breaking on the words, and then he kissed her as her body convulsed around his and the world fell apart and came together again, a more beautiful and perfect whole than ever before.

His words still reverberated through her as she lay in his arms, sated and sleepy. *I love you.* He'd actually said it. But had he meant it? Or had it simply come from the intensity of the moment.

'You're wondering if I meant it, aren't you,' Angelo said softly. He brushed a strand of hair away from her face and Lucia turned to look at him, unable to dissemble.

'Did you?'

'Yes.' He sounded quiet, certain, and yet a little sad. 'Yes, although this is so new for me, Lucia. I've never loved anyone before. I've never let myself.'

'I know,' she said softly.

'But I love you. It doesn't make it easy or comfortable.' He let out a shaky laugh. 'But it feels right. And I can't live without it now. Without you.'

They made love again, even more slowly and languorously this time, and afterwards they showered, washing each other before they made love a third time until Lucia laughed, her face buried in Angelo's neck.

'I'll be exhausted tomorrow.'

'Good thing we can spend the whole day in bed, then.'

'Don't you need to be anywhere?' she asked once they were back in bed, snuggled against each other, this time to sleep. Angelo slid his fingers along hers in turn, not speaking for a moment.

'I can spare a day or two,' he finally said, and Lucia could not keep the disappointment from whispering through her.

'A day or two,' she repeated, and he rolled over to face her.

'This time. But there will be other times and places, Lucia. Other escapes.'

She stared at him, wanting to accept what he said, wanting to believe in it, and yet something held her back. 'What is it?' he asked, and drew her fingers to his lips. 'You're frowning.'

'I don't want a relationship of escapes,' she said after a moment. 'What are we escaping, Angelo?'

He sighed and rolled onto his back, his hand still loosely clasped with hers. 'I didn't mean it like that.'

'How did you mean it?'

'Just…' He shrugged. 'We'll have other holidays. Other cities, other hotels—I want to show you the world.'

'And I want to see it with you,' she said, wishing she could leave it at that, and be content with what they had. Yet she couldn't. That fear still lurked her inside her, whispered its taunts. She knew she wanted to silence that sly voice for ever, and the only way to do that was by speaking it aloud.

'But seeing cities—travelling the world—that's not real life, Angelo.'

'It could be.'

She shook her head. 'What about—what about my life back in Sicily? Your life? What will happen when we return?'

'We can decide what happens. You don't have to return to work as a maid—if you don't want to.'

She knew it cost him to say that, to not demand she quit. He'd never wanted her scrubbing floors, cleaning toilets. And frankly, it wasn't a job she really liked, so why had she clung to it? Out of pride, perhaps, as well as fear. Quitting her job to await Angelo's pleasure felt like the actions of a mistress or a whore, not an equal.

'I don't know what else I would do,' she said after a moment.

'I've been thinking about that. You enjoy helping women like Maria, don't you? With their reading and writing?'

'Yes…'

'Why not start a literacy charity for women like her? Women who had to quit school at sixteen or even younger to work. You could be involved on the ground level, help teach them yourself. I could provide the initial funding—'

She felt an incredulous bubble of hope rise up inside her and she squeezed his hand. 'You would do that for me?'

'Of course I would. And for them, as well. I would have liked to keep at school. I know what it's like to feel frustrated by your own lack of education.'

Softly she kissed his lips. 'You're a good man, Angelo.'

He slid his arms around her and they lay there in silence for a moment, thoughts tumbling through Lucia's mind. *Just leave it*, she told herself. *Leave it and be happy. This is so much more than you ever dreamt of, ever hoped for.* Still she spoke.

'And what about you? When we return to Sicily?'

'What about me?'

She took a breath, prayed for courage to see this through. 'What kind of man will you be, Angelo? Because it's still in your power to decide.'

She felt his emotional withdrawal like a physical thing, as if the very air around them had cooled. He rolled onto his back, slipped his hand from hers. 'I am who I am, Lucia.'

'I know you are, and I love you. But you said yourself how returning to Sicily made you someone you didn't want to be. I don't want you to return and still find you're acting like that person, not when I know who you really are. I know how much goodness you're capable of.'

He stared up at the ceiling, not answering, and Lucia held her breath. He had to see what she meant. He had to give up this awful idea of revenge—

'You're right,' he said at last. 'I don't want to be that boy with a bloody lip and broken dreams. The boy who's always been rejected or reviled. And when I come back to Sicily that's who I feel like, a beggar at the Correttis' feast.' He turned to face her, and determination blazed from his eyes. 'That's why I'm doing this, Lucia. You might see it as some kind of cold-blooded revenge, but it's different than that. I'm showing them—and myself— that I'm not that boy any more. That I'm someone to be reckoned with—' He stopped, his eyes narrowing. 'What?'

Lucia swallowed past the thickening of tears in her throat. 'But, Angelo,' she whispered. 'I fell in love with that boy.'

For a moment she thought he understood. His mouth twisted and she glimpsed that old bleakness in his eyes. Then his mouth firmed and his eyes shuttered. 'Then the question is, do you love the man that boy has become?'

She swallowed again, her throat aching. Everything aching, because she hadn't expected it to come to this so quickly, so terribly. Moments ago they'd been making love. 'I love you, Angelo, but this revenge you're desperate to pursue…it's tearing you—and us—apart. You can't see it, but it is. Why do you think you got that migraine—'

'I've always suffered from headaches.'

'And why do you think that is? Why do you think you still feel so restless and angry, even when you have all the power, all the wealth, you could possibly ever need or want? Why do still feel so empty?'

He stared at her hard, and she thought he might not answer. He might turn away, and then what would she do? How could she make him see how this was destroying him—and any chance their love had?

'Why do you think that is?' he finally asked evenly.

'Because revenge doesn't satisfy you, Angelo. Wealth,

power, any of it—no matter how many companies you buy up, or how many Correttis you grind into the dust, you'll still feel as empty as you did the night of your father's funeral, when you came to me—'

'Don't.'

He rolled away from her, into a sitting position, so she was facing his taut back. Lucia sat up, clutching the duvet to her, knowing they had to have this conversation. The only way was through. 'I must. Our love—any love—can't survive this kind of cold-blooded destruction, Angelo. You have to let it go.'

'It's a business deal, Lucia.'

'No, it's not. It's so much more than that. You might be able to tell Gio Corretti it's just business, but you can't lie to me. You're doing this because you're still the hurt little boy whose father wouldn't acknowledge him, and you hate that.'

'Of course I hate it,' he snapped. He rose from the bed, reached for his trousers. 'You think I want to feel like that again? You think I want to look into the Correttis' sneering faces and see how they've dismissed me?'

'And you think ruining them will achieve anything?'

'Yes—'

'No, Angelo,' Lucia said quietly. 'It won't. It might make them respect you, but that's not what you want.'

'Oh?' He turned to her, dressed only in his trousers, one eyebrow arched in cold incredulity. 'What do you think I want, then?'

'You want them to love you.' She might as well have hit him. He jerked back as if she'd slapped his face. 'And they won't,' she forced herself to continue. 'You can't make someone love you, Angelo. But I love you. I love you with all my heart, and it's love that fills the emptiness, that feeds the hunger. Let my love be enough.'

Angelo didn't respond. He stared at her, his face expressionless, every emotion veiled. Lucia held her breath and waited. What would she do if he said it wasn't?

She would, she realised hollowly, leave him. She would have to.

'Don't make me choose,' he finally said, and it was a warning.

'And if I do?'

'I said, don't make me.'

'Because you will choose revenge.'

'It doesn't have to be like that,' he said, impatient now. He reached for his shirt and shrugged into it. '*Dio*, Lucia, you're the one bent on destruction. Why are you trying to ruin what we have? It's been good so far, hasn't it?'

'It's been amazing,' she whispered. 'It's been the most wonderful experience of my life.'

'So why not just let it go? Why are you always asking for more of me?'

'Because that's what love does, Angelo.' She choked back a sudden sob. 'That's what love is. You don't love half a person. You love all of them, everything, and that's how I want to love you. But I can't—'

'You can't love me if I continue with this?' he finished. 'That sounds like conditional love to me, Lucia. That sounds like you trying to manipulate me as surely as I was trying to when I suggested you become my mistress. I wanted to put you in a compartment of my life, I see that now. In a nice, tidy little box. I wanted to manage you. Now you're doing the same to me.'

'It's not like that,' she insisted. Tears slipped down her face, cold and silent. 'I'm trying to free you from the box you've put yourself in—'

He flung up one hand. 'Enough. I've had enough of

this ridiculous arguing. *Dio*, nothing I ever do will be enough for you.'

'That's not fair. I've never asked for any of this, Angelo. Not the diamonds or the clothes or money or trips to Paris. I just want you. The real you.'

'This,' Angelo said flatly, 'is the real me.' And then he turned and walked out of the room.

CHAPTER TWELVE

ANGELO GAZED MOODILY out the window of his private jet at a grimly cloud-laden sky. The weather had turned grey and cool and after the argument with Lucia last night it suited his mood perfectly. Although if the weather truly suited his mood, a storm would surely be raging, just as anger surged inside him.

Who the hell did she think she was, telling him all that psychobabble? Insisting he wanted the Correttis' *love*? It was absurd, pathetic. Yes, maybe he'd dreamt of such things once upon a time, when he'd been a foolish boy—but now?

Now he wanted revenge. He wanted justice. Didn't she see that? Why couldn't she understand this integral part of himself? And how could she even pretend to love him, when she wouldn't accept this?

Restlessly Angelo settled into his seat. The obvious answer was she didn't love him, never had, just as he'd first thought. She'd convinced herself, perhaps, that she loved him, the him she'd plucked from her own head. He hadn't lived up to that sappy fairy-tale prince, so here he was, flying back to Sicily alone, about to take over more of the Corretti holdings. This morning, after Lucia had left, he'd arranged several private meetings with the shareholders he thought most likely to cave. He could have control of Corretti Designs by this evening. Lucia's leaving had just made him more determined to dominate Corretti Enterprises.

I'll show her.

He stilled in his thoughts, felt his insides curl in something like shame. He sounded like a little boy. He was acting like a little boy…like the little boy she'd claimed he still was, looking for love.

And she gave it to you. She'd asked him to let it be enough, and he'd told her it wasn't. She wasn't.

Resolutely Angelo set his jaw and stared out the window. Lucia had asked too much. He couldn't give up this. He couldn't imagine what life would look like if he did. She wanted to talk about emptiness? He'd be a damn *void* if he let go of this. Of revenge, of proving himself, of finally, *finally*—

Finally what?

Would acquiring one more Corretti company—or two, or a dozen—really make a difference? Would he feel satisfied then, complete? *Happy?*

He sat back in his seat, his jaw bunched so tight his teeth hurt. He knew he wouldn't. And yet even so he could not imagine giving up, letting go—because that thought was still more terrifying than the emptiness he lived with every day.

Lucia gazed around at the tiny bedroom in the hostel near the Gare du Nord where she'd gone after leaving Angelo that morning. It was a far cry from the palatial suite at the Georges Cinq, but it would have to do. It was within her budget, at least.

Angelo, she knew, had been shocked that she had insisted on leaving right then. He'd thought she was making some grand gesture, but it had been simpler, and more awful, than that. She was simply preserving her sanity. She couldn't spend another moment in his company, never mind return to Sicily in his private jet, and not break down. Beg for him to take her back, just as her mother had her father.

How many times had she curled up into a ball in her bed while she heard her mother's noisy sobs from downstairs, her father's gruff replies? And then the slamming of the door, and her father disappeared for a week, a month, however long his money lasted until he was back, to her mother's shaming joy, for more. And then he'd left for good…just as Angelo had.

Except you were the one to leave. You walked away before he could.

A ripple of unease shivered through her, and she tried to shrug it off. She'd made the right decision; she knew she had. As long as Angelo was bent on proving himself in this awful, twisted revenge there was no way a relationship would work. She knew that, had felt it.

And yet—

Did you have to push him so hard? So far? So quickly?

Restlessly Lucia rose from her narrow bed and opened the door. The hallway of the hostel reeked of sweat and boiled vegetables, and she felt as far from home as she ever had. Tears stung her eyes and she blinked them back quickly as she strode towards the front door. Too late for regrets.

She spent the next few hours wandering around Paris, lost in a haze of her own misery and doubt. She could not shake the feeling that she'd made a terrible, terrible mistake.

But what choice had she really had? To go back to Sicily and watch as Angelo ruined the entire Corretti family or died trying? Watch him become more bitter, more determined—and emptier all the while? The end would have happened, sooner or later. She'd just hurried it along.

That's why you pushed him. You were still protecting yourself.

Trust was a choice, and she hadn't trusted. She'd pushed Angelo towards an impossible ultimatum because she was still afraid he was going to walk away. So afraid—and so she'd made him.

She might have told him she was acting out of love, but she hadn't been, not really. She'd been acting out of fear. She'd always been acting out of fear.

Gazing blindly at the Eiffel Tower in the distance, Lucia let out a choked sob. She had made a terrible mistake—and she didn't know how or if she could fix it.

The last of the sun's rays were streaking the sky, and just as before, the moment they'd faded the lights switched on, and the Eiffel Tower shone jewel-bright. She remembered how only last night Angelo had shown her, his eyes warm and bright with love. *I'm so glad I saw it with you.*

Why hadn't she believed in that boy? Why hadn't she given him the time, space and support to make the decision she knew he was capable of? Instead she'd pushed. She'd pushed him away.

And now she needed to get him back.

'It's not that we don't *trust* Luca Corretti—'

'Of course not. This is simply a good business decision.' Angelo smiled coolly at the banker from Milan who would help to orchestrate his insider's coup. With him he could convince the other shareholders to depose Luca as CEO and put him in his place. Corretti Designs would be his. Yet all he could think as he looked at the man's paunchy face was *traitor*.

And all he could feel was emptiness.

He didn't care about Corretti Designs. He knew adding another company to his portfolio wouldn't appease any of the restless emotions inside him, the anger and the hurt and the need.

Only Lucia had done that. Only loving Lucia could do that now.

'Signor…Corretti?' The man stumbled slightly over his name. Angelo lifted his gaze, gave him another cool smile.

'I have the document right here. We need six signatures—half of the board—on it before I can act accordingly.'

'Of course.'

Resolutely Angelo pushed the paper over to the man. He watched him take out his fountain pen, scan the document that would give him control. He thought of Luca's steely authority, the grudging admiration he'd felt for his cousin.

It's not business. Not for you.

No, this had never been about business. Never about money or power or even revenge. It had been, he knew, just as Lucia had told him, about love. About wanting to be loved, accepted—and knowing that the Correttis never would.

But Lucia had. Lucia always had.

'Don't sign.'

The banker looked up in surprise. *'Scusi?'*

'Don't sign.' Angelo smiled grimly. 'I've changed my mind.'

The man's jaw slackened. 'But…the company—'

'Luca Corretti is perfectly capable of turning his company around if need be,' Angelo said. 'I don't need to do it.' He reached for the document and tore it neatly in half. 'I don't need to do any of this.'

With the man still staring at him in slack-jawed amazement Angelo rose from the table. 'And now I'm afraid I must take my leave of you. I have a plane to catch.'

It had taken her the better part of a night and day to get back to Sicily. She didn't have enough money for the airfare, and so she'd taken a train to Milan, another to Genoa and then a twenty-hour ferry to Palermo. By the time she arrived at the hotel she was exhausted, dirty and in desperate need of a bath and a hot meal. She pushed all of it aside in search of the one thing that truly mattered. Angelo.

The bellhops stepped back as she entered, eyes widening in surprise. Perhaps they didn't recognise her as one of the chambermaids, and she certainly didn't look like a guest.

The concierge came hurrying forward. *'Scusi, signorina.'* Her eyes were flinty, her smile perfunctory. 'May I help you?'

'I'm looking for Angelo Corretti.'

'I'm afraid he's not available—'

'I'll just go see for myself.' She strode past the woman who, she could see, was already calling security on a pager. Great. She'd get kicked out of the hotel and fired from her job. So be it. This was more important than any of those things.

She pressed the button for the lift, prayed it would come before security escorted her out. She saw two uniformed men heading towards her just as the doors pinged open—and Angelo stepped out.

The look of incredulous amazement on his face mirrored, she was sure, her own.

'Lucia—'

'*Scusi*, Signor Corretti.' One of the security guards grabbed her arm. 'She just came in—this way, please, *signorina*....'

'Unhand her now.' Angelo's voice was low and deadly and the guards immediately stepped back. 'This woman is not only an employee of this hotel, but my special guest.' He glanced back at her, and his gaze roved hungrily over her face. Lucia felt the first wonderful flare of hope. 'Lucia,' he said softly, urgently, and she swallowed hard.

'Can we...can we go somewhere to talk?'

He nodded, and Lucia started forward. Then he shook his head. 'No, what I need to say to you, I can say here, in front of everyone.'

That didn't sound good. 'But—'

'You were right, Lucia. You were right about everything.'

'Oh, Angelo, I wasn't—'

'I went in pursuit of what I told myself was my dream and I felt only emptier. Lonelier. You're the one who fills me, Lucia. The one who loves me, and I threw the most important thing in my life away with both hands and for what? Just more emptiness. More bitterness.' He shook his head slowly. 'I'm done with it. Done with revenge, done with buying up businesses as a way to change the past or myself or the way others think of me. I'm done with all of it, Lucia.'

'Oh, Angelo.' Tears slipped down her cheeks as she reached for his hands. 'I came here to tell you that I was wrong for pushing you so hard. Forcing you to choose when you weren't ready, when everything between us was still so new. I did it because I was afraid, because even then I was bracing myself for you to walk away from me. If I made you do it, it would be better somehow—but of course it wasn't. It was awful. It was the worst thing in the world.'

'I'm not walking away now,' he told her in a low voice. 'I'll never walk away from you, Lucia. I was a fool to have let you walk away from me. I love you, and I want to live the rest of my life with you, to grow old with you and have more children if you're willing.'

'Yes.' Her throat was so tight she could barely get the word out. 'Yes, I want all of that, more than anything.'

'So do I.' Angelo smiled, his own eyes bright. 'So do I.'

And there, in the middle of the marble lobby of the Corretti Hotel, he sank to one knee, his hand clasped with hers as he looked up at her with love-filled eyes. 'Lucia Anturri, I love you more than life itself. Will you marry me?'

Wordlessly Lucia nodded. Her throat ached too much and her heart was too full to speak. 'Get up,' she finally managed with a tearful laugh. She pulled him to his feet. 'Get up so I can kiss you.'

'I think I can manage that.' Smiling, Angelo drew her into his arms and kissed her soundly, as around them the staff and guests of the Corretti Hotel began to cheer.

* * * * *

*Read on for an exclusive interview
with Kate Hewitt!*

BEHIND THE SCENES
OF SICILY'S CORRETTI DYNASTY:

It's such a huge world to create—an entire Sicilian dynasty. Did you discuss parts of it with the other writers?

Yes, one of the other writers set up an online group where we could discuss continuity points and make sure our stories agreed with one another. It provided a nice sense of community, too, since writing can so often be a lonely business.

How does being part of the continuity differ from when you are writing your own stories?

I think it's always a bit of a jolt when someone else has your hero or heroine as a character in her story. I feel quite possessive of my characters, but it is interesting and fun to see what other writers do with them. Being part of a continuity feels like more of a collaboration than writing on your own, and I enjoy that.

What was the biggest challenge? And what did you most enjoy about it?

The biggest challenge is being given characters and a basic premise that aren't necessarily something you'd think of yourself, and making them your own. It's a challenge I enjoy—and it's a great way to get out of your comfort zone as a writer.

As you wrote your hero and heroine, was there anything about them that surprised you?

They both surprised me. My heroine, Lucia, seemed a bit passive and accepting in the description of her, and yet when I started writing, all this anger and icy control came out, and I realised she was stronger and feistier than I'd been expecting. My hero, Angelo, was focused on revenge, but he surprised me with a softer side, and a longing to be loved he's kept very well hidden.

What was your favorite part of creating the world of Sicily's most famous dynasty?

Both my characters were on the periphery of the family dynasty, so I enjoyed having them carve out their own unique place in the world.

If you could have given your heroine one piece of advice before the opening pages of the book, what would it be?

You are worthy of love and respect, and don't forget it!

What was your hero's biggest secret?

As I mentioned before—his longing to be loved! He wants to seem independent and in need of no one, but no man, after all, is an island, and Angelo wanted to be loved quite desperately.

What does your hero love most about your heroine?

Her faithfulness.

What does your heroine love most about your hero?

His strength.

Which of the Correttis would you most like to meet and why?

I'd like to meet my characters in the flesh—as I think all writers would—and find out what they really think!

COMING NEXT MONTH from Harlequin Presents®
AVAILABLE AUGUST 20, 2013

#3169 CHALLENGING DANTE
A Bride for a Billionaire
Lynne Graham

Dante Leonetti is convinced Topaz Marshall is after his family's money, and he's determined to seduce the truth from her lips. After experiencing Leonetti's ferocious reputation firsthand, will she be able to resist his legendary charms?

#3170 A WHISPER OF DISGRACE
Sicily's Corretti Dynasty
Sharon Kendrick

Rosa Corretti spent one unguarded night with Kulal and now this demanding sheikh wants to control her. The more Rosa resists, the stronger Kulal's desire. But will the arrogant sheikh accept this Corretti for more than one night?

#3171 LOST TO THE DESERT WARRIOR
Sarah Morgan

Desperate to escape an arranged marriage, Layla, Princess of Tazkhan, throws herself at the mercy of Sheikh Raz Al Zahki—her family's greatest enemy! But protection has a price.... This brooding desert king is determined to make her his queen.

#3172 NEVER SAY NO TO A CAFFARELLI
Those Scandalous Caffarellis
Melanie Milburne

Poppy Silverton's home, livelihood *and* innocence are under threat from playboy billionaire Rafe Caffarelli. Poppy will fight Rafe—and her attraction to him—all the way...and be the first woman to say no to a Caffarelli!

You can find more information on upcoming Harlequin® titles, free excerpts and more at www.Harlequin.com.

#3173 HIS RING IS NOT ENOUGH
Maisey Yates

Ajax Kouros has a plan—and being jilted at the altar is *not* part of it. His company's future depends on marrying a Holt, so when his bride's sister steps up to the altar...can he say no?

#3174 CAPTIVATED BY HER INNOCENCE
Kim Lawrence

Cesare Urquart can't possibly believe any worse of Anna Henderson. But when she arrives at his sprawling Scottish estate, Cesare gets a rush of adrenaline he hasn't felt for years and soon questions every notion he's had about her....

#3175 HIS UNEXPECTED LEGACY
The Bond of Brothers
Chantelle Shaw

Sergio Castellano will do whatever it takes to keep the heir he didn't know he had. But the longer he spends with ex-lover Kristen Russell the more he realizes the cracks she once made in his armor are still there.

#3176 A REPUTATION TO UPHOLD
Victoria Parker

When wild and shameless designer Eva St. George is caught with tycoon Dante Vitale it's guaranteed to cause a headline-worthy scandal. But if they can convince the world they're truly in love they might just both get what they want....

HPCNM0813RB

Marcus watched as she got to her feet. He was grateful to see that she was steady.

"Can we have a minute?" Marcus asked Blade.

"Yeah. Hang on to her good arm," his friend replied. Then he walked away, taking Dawson with him.

"What?" she asked, offering him a sweet smile.

"I'm going to find who did this. I promise you. And you're going to be okay. Jamie Weathers is the best emergency physician this side of the Colorado River. Hell, this side of the Missouri River. He'll fix you up. But don't leave the hospital until you hear from me. You understand?"

"I got it," she said. "I'm going to be fine. It's all going to be fine. I barely had twenty bucks in my bag. He didn't even get my phone. I had that in my back pocket. Nor my keys. Those were in my hand. So he basically got nothing except the cash and my driver's license."

Things didn't matter. "You want me to let Brian and Morgan know?"

"Oh, God, no. Please don't do that." She looked panicked. "Morgan can't have stress right now. I'm grateful that her room is on the other side of the building. Otherwise, she could be watching this spectacle."

They would want to know. But it was her decision. And she was in pain. "Okay," he said, giving in easily.

"Thank you," she said.

"Go get fixed up. I'll talk to you soon."

She nodded.

"And, Erin…" he added.

"Yeah."

"I'm really glad that you're okay."

Don't miss
Trouble in Blue *by Beverly Long,*
available March 2022 wherever
Harlequin Romantic Suspense
books and ebooks are sold.

Harlequin.com

HRSEXP0122B